A Girl's Guide to Moving On

"Debbie Macomber's finest novel. Betrayal and sorrow can happen in any stage of life, and, in this wonderful story, her very nimble hands weave a spectacular kaleidoscope of courage, struggles, and finally joyous redemption and reinvention. Macomber totally understands the human heart. I absolutely loved it!"
—Dorothea Benton Frank, *New York Times*
bestselling author of *All the Single Ladies*

"Whispers a message of love, hope, and, yes, reinvention to every woman who has ever wondered 'Is that all there is?' I predict every diehard Macomber fan— as well as legions of readers new to the Macomber magic—will be cheering for Leanne and Nichole, and clamoring for more, more, more."
—Mary Kay Andrews, *New York Times*
bestselling author of *Beach Town, Ladies' Night*,
and *Summer Rental*

"Macomber is a master at pulling heartstrings, and readers will delight in this heartwarming story of friendship, love, and second chances. Leanne, Nichole, Rocco, and Nikolai will renew your faith in love and hope. The perfect read curled up in front of the fire or on a beach, it's as satisfying as a slice of freshly baked bread—wholesome, pleasantly filling, and delicious."
—Karen White, *New York Times*
bestselling author of *Flight Patterns*

"Beloved author Debbie Macomber reaches new heights in this wise and beautiful novel. It's the kind of reading experience that comes along only rarely, bearing the hallmarks of a classic. The timeless wisdom in these pages will stay with you long after the book is closed."
—Susan Wiggs, #1 *New York Times*
bestselling author of *Starlight on Willow Lake*

"Debbie dazzles! A wonderful story of friendship, forgiveness, and the power of love. I devoured every page!"
—Susan Mallery, #1 *New York Times* bestselling author of *The Friends We Keep*

Last One Home

"Fans of bestselling author Macomber will not be disappointed by this compelling stand-alone novel."
—*Library Journal*

"Family, forgiveness and second chances are the themes in Macomber's latest stand-alone novel. No one writes better women's contemporary fiction, and *Last One Home* is another wonderful example. Always inspiring and heartwarming, this is a read you will cherish."
—*RT Book Reviews*

"Tender, real, and full of hope."
—*Heroes and Heartbreakers*

"Once again, Ms. Macomber has woven a charming tale dealing with facing life's hard knocks, begging forgiveness, and gaining self-confidence."
—*Reader to Reader*

"Macomber never disappoints me. . . . She always manages to leave me with a warming of the soul and fuzzy feelings that stay for days." —*Fresh Fiction*

"A very heartwarming novel of healing and reconciliation . . . that touches on life's more serious moments and [will leave readers] hoping to revisit these flawed but lovable characters in the future."
—*Book Reviews & More by Kathy*

Rose Harbor

Sweet Tomorrows

"Macomber fans will leave the Rose Harbor Inn with warm memories of healing, hope, and enduring love."
—*Kirkus Reviews*

"Overflowing with the poignancy, sweetness, conflicts and romance for which Debbie Macomber is famous, *Sweet Tomorrows* captivates from beginning to end."
—*Book Reporter*

"Macomber manages to infuse her trademark humor in a more somber story that focuses on love, loss and faith. . . . This one will appeal to those looking for more mature heroines and a good, clean romance."
—*RT Book Reviews*

"There's a reason why Debbie Macomber is a #1 *New York Times* bestselling author and with *Sweet Tomorrows,* we get another dose of women's fiction perfection. . . . In the nooks and crannies of small-town life, we'll find significance, beauty, and love."
—*Heroes and Heartbreakers*

"Fans will enjoy this final installment of the Rose Harbor series as they see Jo Marie's story finally come to an end." —*Library Journal*

Silver Linings

"A heartwarming, feel-good story from beginning to end . . . No one writes stories of love and forgiveness like Macomber." —*RT Book Reviews*

"Macomber's homespun storytelling style makes reading an easy venture. . . . She also tosses in some hidden twists and turns that will delight her many longtime fans." —*Bookreporter*

"Reading Macomber's novels is like being with good friends, talking and sharing joys and sorrows."
—*New York Journal of Books*

Love Letters

"Macomber's mastery of women's fiction is evident in her latest. . . . [She] breathes life into each plotline, carefully intertwining her characters' stories to ensure that none of them overshadow the others. Yet it is her ability to capture different facets of emotion which will entrance fans and newcomers alike."
—*Publishers Weekly*

"Romance and a little mystery abound in this third installment of Macomber's series set at Cedar Cove's Rose Harbor Inn. . . . Readers of Robyn Carr and Sherryl Woods will enjoy Macomber's latest, which will have them flipping pages until the end and eagerly anticipating the next installment."
—*Library Journal (starred review)*

"Uplifting . . . a cliffhanger ending for Jo Marie begs for a swift resolution in the next book." —*Kirkus Reviews*

"Mending a broken heart is not always easy to do, but Macomber succeeds at this beautifully in *Love Letters*. . . . Quite simply, this is a refreshing take on most love stories —there are twists and turns in the plot that keep readers on their toes—and the author shares up slices of realism, allowing her audience to feel right at home as they follow a cast of familiar characters living in the small coastal town of Cedar Cove, where life is interesting, to say the least."
—*Bookreporter*

"*Love Letters* is another wonderful story in the Rose Harbor series. Genuine life struggles with heartwarming endings for the three couples in this book make it special. Readers won't be able to get enough of Macomber's gentle storytelling. Fans already know what a charming place Rose Harbor is and new readers will love discovering it as well."
—*RT Book Reviews* (4½ stars)

Rose Harbor in Bloom

"Macomber uses warmth, humor and superb storytelling skills to deliver a tale that charms and entertains."
—*BookPage*

"A wonderful reading experience . . . as [the characters'] stories unfold, you almost feel they have become friends." —*Wichita Falls Times Record News*

"[Debbie Macomber] draws in threads of her earlier book in this series, *The Inn at Rose Harbor,* in what is likely to be just as comfortable a place for Macomber fans as for Jo Marie's guests at the inn."
—*The Seattle Times*

"Macomber's legions of fans will embrace this cozy, heartwarming read." —*Booklist*

"Readers will find the emotionally impactful storylines and sweet, redemptive character arcs for which the author is famous. Classic Macomber, which will please fans and keep them coming back for more."
—*Kirkus Reviews*

"Macomber is an institution in women's fiction. Her principal talent lies in creating characters with a humble, familiar charm. They possess complex personalities, but it is their kinder qualities that are emphasized in the warm world of her novels —a world much like Rose Harbor Inn, in which one wants to curl up and stay." —*Shelf Awareness*

"The storybook scenery of lighthouses, cozy bed and breakfast inns dotting the coastline, and seagulls flying above takes readers on personal journeys of first love, lost love and recaptured love [presenting] love in its purest and most personal forms." —*Bookreporter*

"Just the right blend of emotional turmoil and satisfying resolutions . . . For a feel-good indulgence, this book delivers." —*RT Book Reviews* (4 stars)

The Inn at Rose Harbor

"Debbie Macomber's Cedar Cove romance novels have a warm, comfy feel to them. Perhaps that's why they've sold millions." —*USA Today*

"No one tugs at readers' heartstrings quite as effectively as Macomber." —*Chicago Tribune*

"The characters and their various entanglements are sure to resonate with Macomber fans. . . . The book sets up an appealing milieu of townspeople and visitors that sets the stage for what will doubtless be many further adventures at the Inn at Rose Harbor."
—*The Seattle Times*

"Debbie Macomber is the reigning queen of women's fiction." —*The Sacramento Bee*

"Debbie Macomber has written a charming, cathartic romance full of tasteful passion and good sense. Reading it is a lot like enjoying comfort food, as you know the book will end well and leave you feeling pleasant and content. The tone is warm and serene, and the characters are likeable yet realistic. . . . *The Inn at Rose Harbor* is a wonderful novel that will keep the reader's undivided attention." —*Bookreporter*

"Macomber has outdone herself . . . with this heartwarming new series and the charming characters at *The Inn at Rose Harbor*. . . . A wonderful tale of healing and peace." —*The Free Lance–Star*

"*The Inn at Rose Harbor* is a comforting book, one that will welcome readers just as Jo Marie and her inn welcome guests." —*Vibrant Nation*

"A warm and cosy read that tugs at the heartstrings, with love and redemption blooming when it is least expected." —*The Toowoomba Chronicle* (Australia)

"The prolific Macomber introduces a spin-off of sorts from her popular Cedar Cove series, still set in that fictional small town but centered on Jo Marie Rose, a youngish widow who buys and operates the bed and breakfast of the title. This clever premise allows Macomber to craft stories around the B&B's guests, Abby and Josh in this inaugural effort, while using Jo Marie and her ongoing recovery from the death of her husband Paul in Afghanistan as the series' anchor. . . . With her characteristic optimism, Macomber provides fresh starts for both." —*Booklist*

"Emotionally charged romance." —*Kirkus Reviews*

Blossom Street

Blossom Street Brides

"[An] enjoyable read that pulls you right in from page one." —*Fresh Fiction*

"A master at writing stories that embrace both romance and friendship, [Debbie] Macomber can always be counted on for an enjoyable page-turner, and this Blossom Street installment is no exception."
—*RT Book Reviews*

"A wonderful, love-affirming novel . . . an engaging, emotionally fulfilling story that clearly shows why [Macomber] is a peerless storyteller."
—*Examiner.com*

"Rewarding . . . Macomber amply delivers her signature engrossing relationship tales, wrapping her readers in warmth as fuzzy and soft as a hand-knitted creation from everyone's favorite yarn shop." —*Bookreporter*

"Fans will happily return to the warm, welcoming sanctuary of Macomber's Blossom Street, catching up with old friends from past Blossom Street books and meeting new ones being welcomed into the fold."
—*Kirkus Reviews*

"Macomber's nondenominational-inspirational women's novel, with its large cast of characters, will resonate with fans of the popular series." —*Booklist*

"*Blossom Street Brides* gives Macomber fans sympathetic characters who strive to make the right choices as they cope with issues that face many of today's women. Readers will thoroughly enjoy spending time on Blossom Street once again and watching as Lydia, Bethanne and Lauren struggle to solve their problems, deal with family crises, fall in love and reach their own happy endings." —*BookPage*

Starting Now

"Macomber has a masterful gift of creating tales that are both mesmerizing and inspiring, and her talent is at its peak with *Starting Now*. Her Blossom Street characters seem as warm and caring as beloved friends, and the new characters ease into the series smoothly. The storyline moves along at a lovely pace, and it is a joy to sit down and savor the world of Blossom Street once again." —*Wichita Falls Times Record News*

"Macomber understands the often complex nature of a woman's friendships, as well as the emotional language women use with their friends."
—*NY Journal of Books*

"There is a reason that legions of Macomber fans ask for more Blossom Street books. They fully engage her readers as her characters discover happiness, purpose, and meaning in life. . . . Macomber's feel-good novel, emphasizing interpersonal relationships and putting people above status and objects, is truly satisfying."
—*Booklist* (starred review)

"Macomber's writing and storytelling deliver what she's famous for—a smooth, satisfying tale with characters her fans will cheer for and an arc that is cozy, heartwarming and ends with the expected happily-ever-after." —*Kirkus Reviews*

"Macomber's many fans are going to be over the moon with her latest Blossom Street novel. *Starting Now* combines Macomber's winning elements of romance and friendship, along with a search for one woman's life's meaning—all cozily bundled into a warmly satisfying story that is the very definition of 'comfort reading.'" —*Bookreporter*

"Macomber's latest Blossom Street novel is a sweet story that tugs on the heartstrings and hits on the joy of family, friends and knitting, as readers have come to expect." —*RT Book Reviews* (4½ stars)

"The return to Blossom Street is an engaging visit for longtime readers as old friends play secondary roles while newcomers take the lead. . . . Fans will enjoy the mixing of friends and knitting with many kinds of loving relationships." —*Genre Go Round Reviews*

Christmas Novels

A Mrs. Miracle Christmas

"This sweet, inspirational story . . . had enough dramatic surprises to keep pages turning." —*Library Journal*

"Anyone who enjoys Christmas will appreciate this sparkling snow globe of a story." —*Publishers Weekly*

Alaskan Holiday

"Picture-perfect . . . this charmer will please Macomber fans and newcomers alike." —*Publishers Weekly*

"[A] tender romance lightly brushed with holiday magic." —*Library Journal*

"[A] thoroughly charming holiday romance." —*Booklist*

Merry and Bright

"Warm and sweet as Christmas cookies, this new Debbie Macomber romance is sure to be a hit this holiday season." —*Bookreporter*

"Heartfelt, cheerful . . . Readers looking for a light and sweet holiday treat will find it here."
—*Publishers Weekly*

Twelve Days of Christmas

"Another heartwarming seasonal [Debbie] Macomber tale, which fans will find as bright and cozy as a blazing fire on Christmas Eve." —*Kirkus Reviews*

"*Twelve Days of Christmas* is a delightful, charming read for anyone looking for an enjoyable Christmas novel. . . . Settle in with a warm blanket and a cup of hot chocolate, and curl up for some Christmas fun with Debbie Macomber's latest festive read."
—*Bookreporter*

"If you're looking for a quick but meaningful holiday romance that will be sure to spark a need inside you to show others kindness, look no further than *Twelve Days of Christmas*." —*Harlequin Junkie*

"*Twelve Days of Christmas* is a charming, heartwarming holiday tale. With poignant characters and an enchanting plot, Macomber again burrows into the fragility of human emotions to arrive at a delightful conclusion." —*New York Journal of Books*

Dashing Through the Snow

"Wonderful and heartwarming . . . full of fun, laughter, and love." —*Romance Reviews Today*

"This Christmas romance from [Debbie] Macomber is both sweet and sincere." —*Library Journal*

"There's just the right amount of holiday cheer. . . . This road-trip romance is full of high jinks and the kooky characters Macomber does so well."
—*RT Book Reviews*

Mr. Miracle

"Macomber's Christmas novels are always something to cherish. *Mr. Miracle* is a sweet and innocent story that will lift your spirits during the holidays and throughout the year. Celebrating the comforts of home, family traditions, forgiveness and love, this is the perfect, quick Christmas read." —*RT Book Reviews*

"[Macomber] writes about romance, family and friendship with a gentle, humorous touch."
—*Tampa Bay Times*

"Macomber spins another sweet, warmhearted holiday tale that will be as comforting to her fans as hot chocolate on Christmas morning." —*Kirkus Reviews*

"This gentle, inspiring romance will be a sought-after read." —*Library Journal*

"Macomber cheerfully presents a holiday story that combines the winsomeness of a visiting angel (similar to Clarence from *It's a Wonderful Life*) with the more poignant soulfulness of *A Christmas Carol* to bring to life a memorable reading experience." —*Bookreporter*

"Macomber's name is almost as closely linked to Christmas reading as that of Charles Dickens. . . . [*Mr. Miracle*] has enough sweetness, charm, and seasonal sentiment to make Macomber fans happy."
—*The Romance Dish*

Starry Night

"Contemporary romance queen Macomber (*Rose Harbor in Bloom*) hits the sweet spot with this tender tale of impractical love. . . . A delicious Christmas miracle well worth waiting for."
—*Publishers Weekly* (starred review)

"[A] holiday confection . . . as much a part of the season for some readers as cookies and candy canes."
—*Kirkus Reviews*

"A sweet contemporary Christmas romance . . . [that] the best-selling author's many fans will enjoy."
—*Library Journal*

"Macomber can be depended on for an excellent story. . . . Readers will remain firmly planted in the beginnings of a beautiful love story between two of the most unlikely characters."
—*RT Book Reviews* (Top Pick, 4½ stars)

"Macomber, the prolific and beloved author of countless bestsellers, has penned a romantic story that will pull at your heartstrings with its holiday theme and emphasis on love and finding that special someone."
—*Bookreporter*

"Magical . . . Macomber has given us another delightful romantic story to cherish. This one will touch your heart just as much as her other Christmas stories. Don't miss it!" —*Fresh Fiction*

Angels at the Table

"This delightful mix of romance, humor, hope and happenstance is the perfect recipe for holiday cheer."
—*Examiner.com*

Christmas 2019

Dear Friends,

My readers have always been vocal, and I appreciate it. You let me know what you're thinking. Your comments inspire and encourage me. Mrs. Miracle first made her appearance back in the late 1990s and struck a chord with readers. Three Hallmark movies followed. Still, you have let me know you wanted more. This story is the result of your request.

One of the most frequently asked questions I get is what the inspiration is for my stories—where the ideas come from. Most often, they come from life itself or people I meet. In this book, the idea formed when I met Beth Broday, the wife of my film agent. Beth told me the long, difficult journey of the adoption of their daughter. Their story brought tears to my eyes. Later, I met Liberty Lee, the daughter who miraculously came into their lives. It was the miracle part that got my attention and my imagination. Hence, the book you are about to read. I hope you enjoy meeting up with Mrs. Miracle once again. (And just for fun, I threw in a bit of intervention from Shirley, Goodness, and Mercy!) My wish is that my special angels will bring a bit of charm and a smile to your Christmas.

As I stated earlier, my readers are always welcome to contact me. I read every comment and take them to heart. You can reach me through my website or on Twitter, Instagram, or Facebook. If you want to use snail mail, then my mailing address is: P.O. Box 1458, Port Orchard, WA 98366.

The very warmest of holiday greetings,

Debbie Macomber

A Mrs. Miracle Christmas

BALLANTINE BOOKS FROM DEBBIE MACOMBER

A Walk Along the Beach
Window on the Bay
Cottage by the Sea
Any Dream Will Do
If Not for You
A Girl's Guide to Moving On
Last One Home

ROSE HARBOR INN

Sweet Tomorrows
Silver Linings
Love Letters
Rose Harbor in Bloom
The Inn at Rose Harbor

BLOSSOM STREET

Blossom Street Brides
Starting Now

CHRISTMAS NOVELS

A Mrs. Miracle Christmas
Alaskan Holiday
Merry and Bright
Twelve Days of Christmas
Dashing Through the Snow
Mr. Miracle
Starry Night
Angels at the Table

DEBBIE MACOMBER

A Mrs. Miracle Christmas

A Novel

BALLANTINE BOOKS
NEW YORK

A Mrs. Miracle Christmas is a work of fiction. Names, characters,
places, and incidents are the products of the author's imagination
or are used fictitiously. Any resemblance to actual events, locales,
or persons, living or dead, is entirely coincidental.

2020 Ballantine Books Mass Market Edition

Copyright © 2019 by Debbie Macomber
Excerpt from *Jingle All the Way* by Debbie Macomber
copyright © 2020 by Debbie Macomber

Published in the United States by Ballantine Books,
an imprint of Random House, a division of
Penguin Random House LLC, New York.

BALLANTINE and the HOUSE colophon are registered trademarks of
Penguin Random House LLC.

Originally published in hardcover in the United States
by Ballantine Books, an imprint of Random House, a division of
Penguin Random House LLC, in 2019.

This book contains an excerpt from the forthcoming book
Jingle All the Way by Debbie Macomber. This excerpt has
been set for this edition only and may not reflect the
final content of the forthcoming edition.

ISBN 978-0-399-18141-2
Ebook ISBN 978-0-399-18140-5

Cover illustration: Tom Hallman, based on images
© Olga S. Andreeva/Shutterstock (lampposts and water), iStock/
Getty Images Plus (puppy), © MarkWinfrey/Dreamstime.com (house)

Printed in the United States of America

randomhousebooks.com

2 4 6 8 9 7 5 3 1

Ballantine Books mass market edition: October 2020

To Beth Broday and Joel Gotler,
who inspired the story
And to their beautiful daughter,
Liberty Lee

A Mrs. Miracle Christmas

CHAPTER ONE

Laurel McCullough arrived home to find two police cruisers parked in the driveway with their lights flashing. If that wasn't enough to get her heart racing, it was seeing her grandmother on the front porch, clearly distressed, wringing her hands and looking around anxiously.

Laurel slammed her vehicle into park and leaped out of her car, nearly stumbling in her eagerness to find out what had happened.

"Nana," she cried, rushing toward her grandmother.

The instant Laurel came into view, Helen covered her mouth with her hands, and her eyes, filled with dread, looked to the ground.

"Laurel, oh dear, oh dear," she said, her shoulders slumping. "I'm sorry. I've made a terrible mistake."

Laurel wrapped her arms around her grandmother, hoping to comfort her. "Officer, what's going on here?"

"Are you Laurel Lane? This is your grand-mother?"

"Yes, but McCullough is my married name."

"I'm so sorry," Helen repeated, worry lines creasing her face. "When I woke from my nap, my mind was fuzzy. I was afraid because you weren't home from school, so I called the police."

"Your grandmother reported that her ten-year-old granddaughter hadn't returned from school," the kind officer explained to Laurel.

Laurel swallowed down her shock. Nana had been mentally slipping for a while now—little things she couldn't remember, small details—and this was the second major incident within a short time period.

"As you can see, I'm a bit older than ten," Laurel told the officer. "I'm sorry that we've troubled you. She's a bit confused right now. I came to live with my grandmother when I was ten."

"No trouble, Miss. We're just happy we aren't looking at an abduction."

After answering a few more questions for the officers, Laurel gently led her grandmother back into the house and had her sit in her favorite chair.

"I don't know what came over me," Helen said, and moaned, covering her cheeks with her hands. "I'm so embarrassed."

Helen wrapped her arms about herself like she needed to hold on to the present and leave the past behind. "I . . . I looked at the time and you weren't home and suddenly you were ten years old again. I was convinced something dreadful had happened to you. What's wrong with me?" she cried. "How could I have done something so bizarre? Am I going crazy?"

Laurel went to her knees in front of her precious grandmother. "Of course you aren't crazy, Nana. You didn't do anything wrong."

"Those officers came right away and were so kind. I feel terrible to have troubled them." She looked up, seeming to be struck by inspiration. "I should bake them cookies to apologize for wasting their time."

"It's over. I'm home now, and everything is okay."

Laurel brewed tea, thinking it would settle their nerves. She sat beside her grandmother, reassuring her several times.

Laurel's brain raced with how best to deal with this latest situation. Last week, her grandmother had lost her way in the neighborhood, the very one she'd lived in for more than fifty years. Nana had gone out to collect the mail and noticed that the neighbor's new puppy, Browser, had escaped his yard. She'd followed him to try to bring him back and hadn't been able to find her way home. Eventually, the neighbor had found the puppy, along with Helen, and had brought Laurel's visibly upset grandmother back home with her.

Nana looked pale and frightened. "The doctor said that would happen, didn't he? Me getting more and more confused? Wasn't it only last week when I got lost? This is all part of having dementia, isn't it?"

Laurel nodded. The dementia had become significantly worse over the last several months. It was at the point that she didn't feel comfortable leaving her grandmother alone. But what choice did she have? Their financial resources were tight. All she could do was pray that she and Zach, her husband, could come up with a way to manage these new issues that Nana was having.

"I don't want you to worry about me, Laurel," Helen insisted. "I won't be calling the police again, and I won't be going outside on my own anymore, either."

Laurel couldn't bear the thought of her grandmother being stuck inside the house by herself for hours on end, afraid to leave for fear she'd be unable to find her way home.

"You have enough on your plate," Helen continued. "I don't ever want to be a burden."

"You will never be, Nana." Her grandmother had always put others ahead of herself. Laurel set aside her tea and knelt before her nana the way she had as a child. Resting her head in her grandmother's lap, Laurel mulled over this latest development, uncertain what to do.

Helen gently brushed Laurel's hair with her fingers. "You know, I've been praying for you."

Her nana was a prayer warrior. While Laurel wanted to believe God answered prayers, she'd given up all hope. She couldn't help being discouraged. Every road she'd taken to bring a child into their family had turned into a dead end. She couldn't do it any longer. Couldn't hold on to a dream that ended in pain each time. She'd given up and closed the door on the possibility. Laurel had tried to stay positive, but it seemed a baby wasn't ever going to happen for her.

"I guess I should be saying prayers for myself," Nana teased, and gripped hold of her granddaughter's hand. "God has a baby for you. I feel it in my heart, Laurel. Don't give up hope."

Laurel didn't know how to make her nana understand. She and Zach finally had realized that they weren't meant to have children. They'd decided to move forward after coming to terms with their situation. Neither of them was willing to go through yet another failed attempt at the process of bringing a child into their home, into their family. And the sooner Nana accepted that children weren't going to be part of their lives, the better. For her to even mention the possibility of a child pained Laurel.

"Remember Hannah?" Nana reminded her. "She desperately wanted a child, and God gave her Samuel."

Her grandmother was well versed in the Bible and began to recount the stories of other women who had dealt with infertility.

"And Elizabeth, the mother of John the Baptist."

"I do."

"And Rachel."

"Yes, Nana, you've shared these stories with me before," Laurel gently replied. She thought to her-

self that the Bible didn't recount the women who
had been unable to have children.

Her grandmother continued to tenderly brush
Laurel's head. "Don't lose faith, dear one."

It was too late. Tears leaked from Laurel's eyes,
which she hurriedly blinked away. Disappointment
had followed disappointment. The IVF treatments
had been costly in more ways than one. The financial burden was only half of it. The emotional toll
had been devastating. Hope had been shattered with
each negative result, until Laurel had no option but
to abandon her dream of ever being able to give
birth.

While making payments to the fertility clinic,
Laurel and Zach moved in with her grandmother. It
was the only way they could make it financially.
Nana needed them, and they needed her. It was a
win-win for them all.

When the IVF treatments had failed, Laurel and
Zach contacted a reputable adoption agency and
filled out the paperwork. That had been followed by
extensive interviews before they were eventually
placed on a waiting list. A very long list. In fact,
they were informed that it could easily take several
years before they'd be able to receive a baby. Years.
And as each year went by, they knew that their
chances to be chosen to parent an infant would de-
crease.

Month after month followed with no word of a
baby being available. What little hope Laurel had
hung on to dwindled down to a mere speck. She
wanted to believe God heard her prayers—she truly

did. She wanted to think positively, but after years of trying and years of dreaming, only to have those dreams shattered again and again, she found she couldn't. And it wasn't only hope that had diminished; her faith had also hit rock bottom.

Both she and Zach loved children. They would be good parents, and yet they'd been unable to have children of their own. She didn't know where the logic was in this. Why, of all people, had they been denied what they desired the most? It was unfair. Wrong. Devastating.

It was when Laurel was at this low point that Zach had suggested adoption through a fostering program. To her absolute delight, they were given a newborn, a boy, almost immediately. Jonathan had been born to a mother who was addicted to drugs, and he'd been removed from her care. Those first few hellish weeks, the undersized infant had cried incessantly, but Laurel and Zach had stuck it out. They'd loved little Jonathan with all their hearts. Zach had been wonderful with the fussy baby, endlessly comforting him, never growing impatient. He seemed to instinctively know when Laurel needed a break and when to take over. Jonathan responded to Zach's gentle touch and calming voice. Laurel was in awe at what a patient and loving father her husband was.

But then, two weeks before the adoption was to be finalized, Jonathan's birth father had been located. He'd known nothing of the baby and decided he wanted his son. Jonathan had been taken from Laurel and Zach, ripped from her arms. Numb with grief, she'd sunk into a deep depression that had lasted for weeks.

Reeling from the heartache of losing their foster baby, as well as the failed IVF treatments and the endless waiting list from the adoption agency, Laurel decided her heart could endure no more grief. They both agreed it was time to let go and accept that this was the way their lives were meant to be.

"I have the children in my class," she murmured out loud to her grandmother, trying to reassure herself. As a first-grade teacher, Laurel loved every student. Teaching was her calling and her joy, and every day she looked forward to spending time with these precious little ones who were craving to learn.

"You're a wonderful teacher," Nana said. "You'll be an equally fantastic mother."

The front door opened, and her husband called out to announce he was home. Zach was Laurel's rock, her voice of reason, the one who kept her on balance through the worst part of this vicious roller-coaster ride. A computer programmer, he worked at the downtown Seattle offices of Amazon.

He paused when he saw Laurel on the floor in front of her grandmother. Alarmed, his eyes quickly met Laurel's.

Scrambling to her feet, Laurel stood and hugged her husband, loving the solid feel of his body against hers. "It's been quite the day." She hated to hit him with unwelcome news the instant he walked in the door. "Did you happen to see the police cars leaving the neighborhood on your walk home from the bus stop?"

Perplexed, Zach said that he had.

"I'm afraid I'm the culprit," Helen announced. "I called the police because I thought Laurel had been kidnapped."

"What?" Zach burst out.

"It's all been taken care of," Laurel hurried to say, not wanting to upset her grandmother further. "Just a misunderstanding."

"I forgot that Laurel is an adult," Nana explained to Zach. "In my mind she was still a schoolgirl, and she wasn't home from school, and I got worried, so I called the police, and they came, and . . . oh dear, I've really made such a mess of things, haven't I?"

Zach gently touched her shoulder and looked lovingly into Helen's eyes. "Are you okay? That's all that matters."

"Yes, yes, I'm fine. I feel so foolish."

His brow furrowed and he shared a worried look with Laurel. "Let's just be glad everything turned out okay. What's for dinner?" He looked over at his wife. This was a code the two shared that meant they needed to talk privately.

"Meat loaf," Laurel said, heading toward the kitchen. "I need to get it in the oven."

"I'll help," Zach said, following close behind.

The minute they were sure Nana couldn't hear their discussion, he expressed his concern. "What was Helen thinking calling the police?"

"I know. And it was only last week when she got lost in her own neighborhood. What are we going to do?"

Sinking into a kitchen chair, Zach folded his

hands, a habit he had when deep in thought. "This can't continue. We need to bring someone in."

"But who?"

"There are agencies that provide this kind of care. It's time we looked into it."

Neither of them dared to mention the expense. Somehow, they'd make it work. They both knew that Nana wouldn't do well in an assisted-living facility. She was most comfortable in her own home, surrounded by all that was familiar and by those she loved.

Laurel lowered herself into the chair across the table from her husband. Her heart sank as she shared more unfortunate news. "Nana called me Kelly last week."

Zach placed his hand over Laurel's, giving it a gentle squeeze.

Kelly was Laurel's mother, who had died in a freak accident when Laurel was ten. Her mother had slipped on the ice, hit her head, and died shortly afterward. Laurel's father, Michael, regularly traveled out of state as a business consultant, and, unable to change his work commitments, he reluctantly sent Laurel to live with her grandparents. Eventually, her father had remarried and moved to another state with his new wife. Rather than uproot Laurel, he knew it was best for his daughter to stay with her grandparents. Laurel's relationship with her father remained close, and they'd talked almost every night. He'd always stop by to visit when he was in the Seattle area, and she spent many school breaks with him and his new family. Laurel never doubted her father's love and was grateful that he'd seen the wisdom of keeping her with her grandparents.

"I'll research a few different home-care agencies tonight and give them a call before school starts in the morning," Laurel said. Zach was right. The dementia was getting worse. They couldn't risk leaving Helen alone any longer.

At dinner that evening, Helen pushed the food around on her plate, showing no interest in her meal.

"Don't you like the meat loaf?" Laurel asked. Her grandmother seemed to have lost her appetite lately, and the weight loss was evident in the way her clothes hung on her body.

"It's good, but I'm not hungry. If it's all right, I think I'll head to bed early."

"But *Wheel of Fortune* is on." It was her grandmother's favorite show. Nana had watched it for as long as she could recall, and for her to miss it was yet another unwelcome sign for Laurel.

"The puzzles have become too hard. I used to be good at figuring them out. I seem to have lost my touch."

Zach shared a look with Laurel.

"Would you like me to read to you?" Laurel asked her grandmother.

Again, Nana wasn't interested. "Another time."

While Zach cleaned the kitchen, Laurel helped her grandmother get ready for bed. Lately, Nana seemed to require more sleep and was often still in bed when Laurel left for school in the morning. Laurel attributed it to the medication Dr. Fredrickson had recently prescribed for her grandmother. Long sleeping patterns was only one of the drug's side effects. It also caused vivid dreams that often left Nana disturbed.

The following day, Laurel placed a call to the first agency on her list to see about hiring a home companion to stay with her grandmother while she and Zach were at their respective jobs.

"I wish I had someone," the woman from Caring Angels said, introducing herself as Elise Jones. "Unfortunately, every one of the caretakers in our agency is already out on assignment."

"Oh dear." This wasn't the news that Laurel wanted to hear.

"I'd be happy to put your name on a waiting list."

Laurel was already sadly familiar with waiting lists. The idea of being placed on another made her cringe. "Do you have any idea how long it will take before you have someone available?"

The woman hesitated. Laurel could hear the clicking of her computer keys in the background. She didn't know how much longer she could wait. The situation with her grandmother was quickly becoming critical.

"I can't see anything opening up before the first of the year."

"That long?" *Another month,* Laurel thought to herself. All she could do was hope that someone would become available sooner, rather than later.

The one bright spot was that with Christmas nearly upon them, she'd be home from school for a couple weeks around the holidays. Thankfully, she wouldn't need to return until after the first of the year.

"Should I put your name on the list?"

Seeing that she had no other option, Laurel agreed. "Please."

After giving the agency all the pertinent information, Laurel hung up the phone and called two other agencies. They had longer waiting lists than the Caring Angels agency. She phoned Zach to give him the news.

"What did you find out?" he asked.

"We're on a waiting list. They expect to have someone available after the first of the year."

Zach didn't hide his concern. "Do you think she'll be all right by herself until your Christmas break?"

"Do we have a choice?"

"I guess not," Zach said, sounding as defeated as Laurel felt.

"I can always drive home to check on her during my lunch," Laurel said, although she wasn't sure how that would work. If she got caught up in traffic and was late returning, it would cause major problems, possibly even the loss of her job. She couldn't leave the children unattended, and staffing was so tight that it was unfair to ask someone to watch her class until she got back. It didn't help that she had signed up to organize the Christmas program at school.

How did my life get so complicated? Laurel pondered. Yet she knew in her heart that she would never ignore her grandmother's needs. Nana had been there for Laurel when she'd needed her the most, and Laurel was determined to do the same for Nana.

At the end of the school day, Laurel hurried home without staying to do her normal paperwork, afraid to leave her grandmother alone any longer than necessary. To add to her list of things to be done that evening, Laurel had intended to bake cookies for the small party the staff was throwing for the main-office secretary's birthday. A week earlier, Laurel had bragged about her grandmother's recipe for snickerdoodles, and she'd been volunteered.

When Laurel came through the door, she found Nana sitting in her favorite chair, watching a rerun of *Antiques Roadshow,* with her fingers busily knitting. As a matter of habit, her grandmother usually picked up her needles and yarn at least once a day, but as of late, she was making little to no progress on any particular project. Helen looked up and smiled. Laurel noticed that she looked better than she had the previous day.

"You're home from school already?" Nana asked, surprised at Laurel's earlier arrival time.

Hanging up her coat, she sat down near her grandmother, pleased to see that she was looking more like herself. "What are you working on?"

Her grandmother stared down at the yarn for a long moment.

"Hmm, let me think. It doesn't come to mind right away, but don't you just love the yarn?"

Laurel patted her hand. "Don't worry, Nana. It's not important. The yarn is gorgeous, and so soft."

Zach returned home a little more than an hour and a half later, and together, the three sat down for dinner. Just as Laurel was about to take her last bite from her meal, the doorbell chimed. Zach looked at Laurel and she at him.

She shrugged in response. "I'm not expecting anyone. Are you?"

"Nope. I'll get it." Zach slid back his chair and headed to the front door.

Laurel watched from the kitchen. An older woman stood on the other side of the threshold. She was dressed in a full-length wool coat with a thick scarf wrapped around her neck. She carried a basket on her arm and had a wide smile on her face.

"Good evening," she greeted cheerfully. "I'm Mrs. Miracle."

"Mrs. Miracle," Zach repeated, sounding puzzled. "How may I help you?"

"I believe I'm here to help *you*. I understand you put in a request for a Caring Angel."

CHAPTER TWO

"Caring Angels sent you?" Laurel asked, coming out of the kitchen after she had overheard the initial exchange. "When I called earlier, I was told no one was available."

"The office hadn't been informed that I was free to accept another assignment. When I heard your situation was urgent, I came as quickly as I could. I trust I haven't arrived at a bad time?"

"No, of course not. Please come in." Looking relieved and grateful, Laurel quickly brought the older woman into the house.

Helen sat quietly, observing the arrival of this stranger. She sensed an immediate connection to this woman who had entered her home, yet she couldn't understand why. It appeared that she and this Mrs. Miracle weren't far apart in age. Somehow, though she couldn't explain it, Helen instinctively knew that this woman had a warm heart, and that the two of them would get along famously.

"The agency said that you sounded quite desperate. The instant she discovered I was free to take on a new client, she gave me the referral. I hope I'm not interrupting your dinner."

"No, no," Laurel quickly reassured her. "We are all finished." Laurel offered Mrs. Miracle tea or coffee, which she politely refused.

"You're an answer to our prayers," Helen said, still seated in her chair.

"I'm often told that," Mrs. Miracle said. "But really, being a Caring Angel is my privilege. I enjoy the work."

Helen could see the relief in her granddaughter's eyes. She felt dreadful for causing such concern recently for Laurel and Zach and was determined to do everything she could to keep things straight. No more police, and no more getting lost, that was for sure.

In a businesslike fashion, Mrs. Miracle got right to work. "I understand you both have jobs outside of the home, so I brought the paperwork from the agency for you to sign."

Zach reached for the folder the caregiver handed him.

"No need for you to take time off work to come downtown to meet anyone, as you've already been introduced to Caring Angels over the phone. Once the paperwork is signed, I'll hand it off."

"Thank you. That's thoughtful of you," Laurel said.

Mrs. Miracle looked toward Helen and winked. They shared a smile, and Helen was left to wonder what the wink was all about. She couldn't keep from smiling and winking back at her new caretaker.

Zach looked up from the paperwork, his eyes full of surprise and relief. "This is far less expensive than we'd anticipated."

"It's the holiday special," Mrs. Miracle explained. "Oh—and before I forget—I brought you a little something." She set her basket on the coffee table and removed the red-checkered cloth covering it. "I like to bring a homemade item to my new clients on my first in-home visit. I enjoy baking and have several wonderful holiday recipes."

Helen leaned forward to peek. "You brought us cookies?"

"These happen to be my personal favorites," Mrs. Miracle said. "I dare not keep them around, otherwise I'd be tempted to eat the entire batch myself."

Helen removed a large plate of snickerdoodles.

"Snickerdoodles," Laurel said, a bit taken aback. "You brought us snickerdoodles? Nana was right. You *are* an answer to our prayers."

"Yes, dear. I get that a lot." With that comment, Mrs. Miracle stood and collected the signed paperwork from Zach. "I don't mean to rush off, but I need to be on my way. What time would you like me to arrive in the morning?"

"Is eight too early?" Laurel asked.

"Not in the least." Walking over to Helen, the

caregiver reached down and took Helen's hand in hers. "We're going to be the best of friends."

Helen felt a warmth spread down her arm and into the rest of her body with the tender gesture from Mrs. Miracle. "I believe we will."

"Now you sleep well, dear, and I'll see you first thing in the morning. We'll enjoy getting to know each other tomorrow."

"I can't wait." She'd felt drawn to the caregiver and had liked her immensely after only a few minutes.

Zach walked Mrs. Miracle to the door and saw her out. When he returned, Laurel seemed giddy with relief. "She's wonderful. I can't believe how lucky we are to have her, and so soon."

"She brought *cookies*. Who does that?" Zach asked.

Helen smiled, seeing that a great burden had been lifted off her granddaughter's shoulders. Zach had easily been won over, and all it'd taken was a few warm snickerdoodles. Helen wondered why neither of them had asked many questions of this stranger who was now to be her caretaker. It was like this woman had some sort of strange power over them all.

Helen's mind was fuzzier with each passing day, and while she did her best to hide it from Laurel and Zach, it was becoming next to impossible. It deeply distressed her that she had mistakenly thought Laurel was still a ten-year-old. Helen feared the day would come when she'd forget her own name. Or that of her beloved granddaughter. Somehow, though, she felt a new sense of optimism rising inside her.

That night she fell deeply asleep, the best night of sleep she'd had in ages.

When Helen awoke the following morning, her granddaughter was dressed and ready to head off to school. Helen rarely saw Zach on weekday mornings, as he'd leave before she got up.

At precisely five minutes to eight, the doorbell rang, and Laurel greeted Mrs. Miracle at the door. The caregiver wore the same full-length coat and scarf, which she promptly removed as she stepped in.

"Good morning, Helen," she said, with a surprising amount of energy. "It's a new day, and we're going to have fun!"

Mrs. Miracle's enthusiasm filled Helen.

Turning to Laurel, Mrs. Miracle added, "Don't you worry about a thing, Laurel. Would you like me to prepare dinner for your family before you arrive home?"

"You prepare meals, too?"

"Oh yes, like I mentioned last night, I enjoy cooking."

"There's a roast in the freezer. I'll get it out for you." With her hands clasped, Laurel looked upward toward the ceiling. "I think I'm in heaven."

Mrs. Miracle laughed. "You're not there quite yet, my dear. Now off to work. I don't want you to be late. I'll prepare Helen's breakfast and then the two of us can plan our day's adventures."

"If you have a problem or need anything, my work number is on the bulletin board in the kitchen, as well as my cellphone number, although I won't be able to answer unless I'm on a break."

"We'll be perfectly fine. Don't forget the cookies."

"Oh my goodness. I nearly did." Laurel raced back to the kitchen, then hesitated on her way out the door. "How did you know I needed to take these snickerdoodles to school?"

Mrs. Miracle shrugged. "You must have mentioned it last night."

"I did?" Laurel frowned in thought. "I don't recollect saying anything about it."

"You did, dear. Otherwise, how would I have known?"

Laurel hesitated, letting Mrs. Miracle's reply sink in for a moment before she nodded. "Right." And with that simple agreement, she was out the door.

Returning to her bedroom, Helen intended to dress for the day, but she couldn't recall what day it was. If it was Sunday, she would choose a dress. Monday was laundry day, but this wasn't Monday, was it? She stood in front of her closet for several minutes, unsure of what to do. It wasn't long before Mrs. Miracle joined her.

"It's Wednesday," she said to Helen, taking out a pair of navy-blue pants and a warm, off-white sweater for her.

"It's winter?" Helen could have sworn it was spring.

"December."

"Christmastime?" Helen asked.

"Yes, Christmas will be here soon."

While Helen finished dressing, Mrs. Miracle prepared a breakfast of toast and cooked oatmeal with raisins. It was ready for Helen when she came down the stairs. She stared at the spread as a wealth of childhood memories suddenly flooded over her. Oatmeal was standard fare for breakfast when she was a child. Her mother added raisins as a special treat. The family had lived in North Dakota, where the winters were harsh and bitter. Oatmeal had always warmed her stomach before she raced out of the house to catch the school bus.

"My brother would give me his raisins," Helen murmured out loud, recalling the day James scooped all the raisins out of his oatmeal for her, after she'd helped him with his math homework.

"James never was good with numbers, was he?"

"No. But that didn't hold him back. He was a real people person and went on to sell tractors. He did well for himself. He had a way with nearly everyone and could talk about anything. My dad said James could tell folks that the sky was green and the grass was blue in such a way that they'd believe him."

"That he could," Mrs. Miracle concurred.

Helen cocked her head to one side. "You knew my brother?"

"We've met."

Helen was confused, but this wasn't the same kind of confusion she usually felt. This was different. Her dear brother had died of a heart attack when he was in his forties. It had nearly killed her parents to lose their youngest child.

"My brother died over twenty-five years ago."

"Yes, I know," the caregiver said, finishing the dishes.

"When did you meet him?"

She continued to scrub the oatmeal pan. "It was recently, just before I took this assignment. I like to know as much as I can about those who Gabriel assigns to me."

"Gabriel?" Helen was filled with questions. Who was Gabriel? And how was it possible that Mrs. Miracle had talked to her brother? This couldn't be right. She might forget certain things, but she was confident Mrs. Miracle couldn't have met her brother.

"He sends his love," the caregiver added, "and he wanted you to know that he's sorry that he lost your bicycle."

Helen gasped. This was a story from her childhood. Because his bicycle had a flat, James had taken hers without asking. While hanging out with his buddies in the local park, the bike had been stolen, and he'd never told anyone. Years later, as an adult, James finally admitted to Helen that he was the one responsible for the loss of her precious bike.

This was all so strange. It made no sense. Only someone from the other side of life could've possibly communicated with her brother. She looked up from the table and stared at the caregiver with fresh eyes. As a believer, she was convinced of a spiritual realm, and now she felt like she had living proof in front of her.

"Mrs. Miracle . . ." She hesitated, afraid to say the words, fearing the other woman would find the question far-fetched and ridiculous.

"Yes?" Mrs. Miracle waited expectantly.

"Are you . . ." Helen straightened her shoulders, wanting answers. "Who sent you?"

A big smile came over the caregiver's face. "You mean you don't know?"

This woman was going to make Helen say the words that were in her head. "When you said Gabriel gave you this assignment, are you . . . are you telling me it was the *angel* Gabriel?"

The question hung in the air. "Are *you* an angel?"

Mrs. Miracle's entire face glowed.

Helen shook her head, needing to clear her thoughts. "Where are your wings? Aren't you supposed to have a pair of wings and dress in a white robe?"

Mrs. Miracle laughed heartily. "Oh heavens, no. Can you imagine the ruckus I'd cause if I walked down the street in that getup?"

"But . . ."

"I'm a different sort of angel, a Caring Angel."

That name was familiar. Helen recalled that it was the name of the home-companion agency. She tried to make sense of all this new information. "Are all the home companions from the agency angels like you?" Surely someone would have figured it out before now, she reasoned. This would have been big news, broadcast around the world.

"No, just me. I came here especially for you."

Helen's hand flew to her chest. "For me? Why me?"

"My dear," Mrs. Miracle explained, "you've been praying, and God heard your prayers. He sent me to be with you."

Still skeptical, Helen felt the need to find out more. "That's all well and good, and please don't think I'm being ungrateful, but my prayers have been for my granddaughter, not for me."

"Yes. Yes, I know."

"Her faith is weak, and who can blame her? My Laurel has been through so much."

"I know all about your granddaughter and her husband's trials to start a family."

That Mrs. Miracle knew this shouldn't have surprised Helen, if indeed she was an angel. But it sure seemed to Helen that this woman was privy to a lot of personal information, angel or not.

"Laurel might have lost her faith," the caregiver continued, "but you haven't. You've kept on trusting and praying."

Helen had relentlessly prayed for her granddaughter and her husband, Zach. Her heart had broken for them when they'd had no choice but to relinquish Jonathan to his birth father. Helen had watched her granddaughter's faith crumble once the baby had been removed from their home. But Helen had refused to stop petitioning God on behalf of her granddaughter, or to let go of the dream she had of seeing her great-grandchild in Laurel's arms.

Helen's heart beat hard and fast to the point that

she was afraid she might faint. "With you coming to take care of me . . . does that mean Laurel and Zach are going to have a baby?"

"I wouldn't be here otherwise," Mrs. Miracle confirmed. "A special baby girl is about to be born, and that baby is meant for your granddaughter and her husband."

"Oh, thank you, thank you," Helen replied, tears of joy filling her eyes. "But why did God have Laurel wait for so long?" Despite her fading memory, Helen would never forget holding her granddaughter closely as she wept tears of loss and discouragement after each failed fertility treatment. Helen had felt inadequate, wanting desperately to comfort the precious granddaughter she'd raised. She knew the pain had cut deep into Laurel's soul.

Pulling out the chair and sitting down across from Helen, Mrs. Miracle gently took her hands. "The baby hasn't arrived yet, but she will be here soon. You'll get to see Laurel with her baby, and witness her happiness, all in due time."

Tears of joy filled Helen's eyes, and she wanted to ask more, but she was interrupted.

"But enough of what the future holds for Laurel and Zach. Time to focus on you. You've got some knitting to do, and while we're working, let's make a list of things you'd like to do now that you have me by your side."

The unbelievably great news carried Helen all throughout the rest of the day. The hours slipped by quickly as the two women knitted, made plans, and got to know each other better.

———

Dinner was roasting in the oven when Laurel arrived home from her day at school.

"Whatever you're cooking, it smells divine," she said, shrugging off her coat and hanging it in the hallway.

"It's an old family recipe from way back. I believe I got it from Eve," Mrs. Miracle explained, crossing paths with Laurel as she headed for the door for her scarf and coat.

Laurel didn't question the comment, although Helen was certain the "Eve" that Mrs. Miracle had mentioned quite possibly had been married to an "Adam."

"You're welcome to stay and eat with us, if you'd like," Laurel said before she walked over to kiss her grandmother's cheek. "Did you have a good day, Nana?"

"You wouldn't believe the fun we had!"

"I appreciate the offer," Mrs. Miracle said, "but I need to head home."

"Of course." Laurel followed her to the front door and saw her out.

The two talked on the front porch for a few moments before Mrs. Miracle left. Laurel returned to her grandmother's side, looking relaxed and at ease.

"How was your day at school?" Helen was ready to burst with the news of what she'd learned from the caregiver.

"Wonderful." Laurel sat on the ottoman in front of Helen's chair. "I've been working with my class, getting them ready for the holiday program. Their performance is scheduled right before the holiday break."

Helen couldn't stay quiet a moment longer. "I have a secret," she whispered, looking both ways before she continued. "A wonderful secret."

"Do share," Laurel whispered back, her eyes brightening.

"Mrs. Miracle is a Caring Angel."

"Yes, Nana, I know."

"I mean . . . she's a *real* angel."

"A real angel?" A frown started to form on Laurel's face.

"Yes. *God* sent her."

Laurel's look went from one of puzzlement to one of concern.

"You have to believe me, Laurel."

"I agree with you, Nana; she's a wonderful, highly qualified Caring Angel from the agency I contacted."

"And there's more, so much more, I have to tell you, and I will, but not yet."

"Nana?"

"Don't look so concerned," Nana said, clapping her hands together. "Oh, this is going to be the very best Christmas yet!"

CHAPTER THREE

With her mind whirling, Laurel headed to the kitchen, anxious for Zach to get home from work. This latest development in her grandmother's mental stability was deeply concerning. That her grandmother would seriously believe her new caretaker was an actual living and breathing angel provided Laurel with stark, sad proof of how far Nana's mental condition had deteriorated.

"Doesn't that roast smell intoxicating, Laurel? Mrs. Miracle said she'd share the recipe, if you wanted." Her grandmother's voice dipped. "Like she said, this recipe has been handed down through the generations."

Laurel was so deep in thought that the offer went unanswered.

"Laurel, did you hear me?"

"Sorry, Nana, I was daydreaming. Yes, I'd love the recipe."

"I thought you would. I'll ask Mrs. Miracle to write it down for you."

Her grandmother sounded so cheerful. Laurel hadn't seen her this happy in several weeks. Laurel had to believe it was due to having someone at home with her all day now. After one day, Mrs. Miracle was already making a difference. Laurel knew her grandmother had been lonely during the day, and she had instant regret that she and Zach hadn't tried this sooner. Mrs. Miracle, angel or not, seemed to be an answer to their prayers.

"How's the holiday program coming along at school?"

"The children are quickly learning the song." The first-grade classes' part was adorable. Laurel was convinced they would be the hit of the show, singing a familiar, upbeat Christmas carol. Six-year-old Priscilla, one of her students, was a wiggle worm and couldn't stand still when she started singing. Her arms and legs moved the entire time, bouncing to the beat of the music. It distracted the other children, but Laurel didn't have the heart to discourage the little girl's enthusiasm. She was the sweetest child, full of spunk and energy. Each one of Laurel's students held a special place in her heart.

"Tell Mrs. Miracle the snickerdoodles were a huge hit at the birthday party. Everyone raved about them."

"She gave you snickerdoodles? Oh yes, that's right. Do you want me to see if she'll share that recipe, too?"

"I'd like that, Nana."

"Mrs. Miracle is a knitter—did I mention that?"

"Ah, no . . ."

"Working alongside her has helped me to remain more focused on what I'm knitting. It's been quite some time since I finished anything, and I can't believe how fast my fingers fly when I'm knitting next to her."

This was welcome news. Laurel had watched her nana's life narrow down to doing little more than sitting in front of the television set and aimlessly knitting a couple of rows. Day after day it was the same thing. The big excitement of Helen's life had become the weather report. The interests she'd once enjoyed had slowly faded away one by one. She no longer met with friends at the senior center or participated in the church prayer-shawl ministry. Several of her dearest friends had died. Nana had all but given up cooking for fear she might inadvertently forget to turn off the burner.

"It's wonderful that you have someone to knit with, Nana." Laurel was enthused. This was exactly the kind of thing she'd hoped would happen. "What did you start on?"

Nana fidgeted, acting like the question made her uncomfortable.

"You don't need to tell me if you prefer not to." Maybe it was a Christmas gift, so Laurel didn't want to press her. Over the years, Laurel had been gifted with beautiful shawls, scarves, and afghans that her grandmother had knit. Nana used to fly through yarn and patterns. A project had always been on her needles.

"Oh, it's fine, dear. I was saving it as a surprise, but it won't do any harm to tell you. I'm knitting a pair of booties for when your adoption comes through."

Laurel instinctively turned away and closed her eyes until the sting passed. Her grandmother had no idea the pain her words caused. Her remarks were like rubbing a fresh lemon over a wound—an injury that remained open and raw from losing Jonathan.

Her gaze shot to the closed bedroom door, Jonathan's nursery. She'd closed that door in more ways than one and demanded that it remained closed. Both Nana and Zach had abided by her wishes. The room was essentially sealed off and left exactly as it was from the day Jonathan had been taken from them. No one had set foot inside it since then.

"Let me know if you need help with dinner," Nana said cheerfully, as she settled back into her favorite chair to watch the early-evening news. "We set the table already."

Laurel pulled the roast out of the oven and set it on top of the stove. Zach was due home anytime now. She hadn't expected Mrs. Miracle's willingness to cook for the family, and having the meal ready was a real treat.

Soon, Laurel heard Zach cheerfully greeting Nana. After dispensing with his coat and bag, he joined Laurel in the kitchen. Wrapping his arms around her waist, he pulled her close and kissed her. It was more than a peck on the cheek—it was a kiss generally reserved for times when they were alone.

"Wow," she whispered when he released her. "You must have had a really good day at the office."

"I had a great day."

"Did you get a promotion? A raise?"

"None of the above," he said. "No real reason, I suppose, other than I was busy, and the hours flew by. You know I love my job, and any day I can come home to my beautiful wife, I feel lucky." He reached into the pan on the stove and pinched off a piece of the tender meat.

"Be careful, that's hot," Laurel warned.

"I see that," he said, licking his fingertips. "Wow, that's good. How did the first day go with Nana and the home companion?"

"I came home to a different grandmother than I've seen in quite some time: She was working on a knitting project, wanting to share every detail of her day with me, and even interested in watching the evening news. But we need to talk," Laurel said, lowering her voice. She didn't want her grandmother to overhear their conversation.

"What's up?"

"It's Nana."

"But I thought you just said she had a great day. What's wrong?"

Laurel drew in a breath and whispered, "Nana believes her new caretaker is an angel."

"Well, yes, she's a Caring—"

"A *real* angel," Laurel interrupted, "as in the heavenly type . . . one sent from God."

"Oh." Zach's eyes enlarged. "She actually said this?"

Nodding, Laurel explained. "The minute Mrs. Miracle left, Nana was fairly bursting to share the news with me. I haven't seen her this excited since we told her we'd decided to move in with her."

Zach walked from one end of the kitchen to the other, and then back again, needing time to process this latest development in Helen's mental decline.

"How did you respond?" he asked.

"What could I say?" Laurel said, gesturing helplessly with her hands. "I didn't want to argue with her. This worries me, Zach."

"Yes," he agreed, "that is troublesome."

"What should we do?"

Her husband held her look for several seconds. "Why say anything? If Nana wants to believe her caretaker is a real angel, then let her. I don't see how it will do any harm."

Laurel wasn't as sure. "You don't?"

"Really, Laurel, think about it. Minutes ago, you told me how well Nana did today. It's like she's back to her old self. In my opinion, if she wants to believe her caregiver is an angel in human form, then what good would it do to try to convince her otherwise?"

He was probably right, and she slowly nodded.

"Okay," Laurel said, "we'll go along with her on this and let her believe what she wants."

Sure enough, as soon as the three sat down for dinner, Nana started in about angels.

"Gabriel sent Mrs. Miracle to us," she said, looking at Zach. "I suppose Laurel told you everything?"

Zach winked at Laurel. "She might have mentioned it."

"Oh, good. You can imagine how surprised I was to learn this. And there's more."

"More?"

"Yes," she said excitedly. "She's come as an answer to my prayer, but there's no need to go into that just now."

"Did she give you specific details?" Zach asked.

"Not yet, but I'm sure she will."

Laurel watched as Zach went along with her grandmother's story. She could tell he was amused, but not to the point of making fun of her nana. Zach had loved Helen from the minute he met her, and they shared a special bond.

"I can't wait to hear more," he replied, sharing a smile with Laurel.

Helen had a hearty appetite, which was unlike her these days. Laurel and Zach were pleasantly surprised.

"I had such a wonderful day," Nana said with a sigh. "It was so good to hear about my brother."

"Uncle James?" Laurel asked.

Nana passed the cooked carrots and potatoes on to Laurel and continued her story. "Mrs. Miracle told me he's doing well in heaven. That's reassuring. My brother was such a prankster."

"Yes, Nana," Laurel said, the smile fading from her face. This was getting to be more than just her grandmother believing that her caregiver came from heaven.

"Mrs. Miracle knew all about him."

"Did she, now?" Zach said, sharing a concerned glance with Laurel.

"Oh yes. We had quite the gabfest about him."

"That's great," Zach said. "Tell me more."

Nana excitedly shared the story, more animated than Laurel had seen her in a very long while.

Kicking Zach's leg under the table, Laurel glared at him. She was starting to think that they shouldn't be encouraging Nana with this line of thought. Her grandmother was losing sight of reality. While she agreed that they shouldn't argue with Nana or point out that it was a fantasy, they shouldn't encourage her.

Laurel didn't get a chance to speak to him privately until they were getting ready for bed. "You can't go along with her wild imagination, Zach," she said, wanting to clear the air. "While I'm pleased that Nana is showing improvement, I'm afraid it's going too far. I saw her show you the baby booties she's knitting." Zach seemed to be playing along with Nana more than Laurel was comfortable with. He, too, seemed to be living in the fantasy world right along with Nana, and it distressed Laurel. At least one person in this house needed to be living in reality.

"What about the booties?" Zach challenged.

The last thing Laurel wanted was for them to argue. The subject of a baby was taboo. He knew that. She offered him a shallow smile. "I don't think it's a good idea to encourage her along those lines."

"Why not?" he asked.

"You know why not."

She shouldn't have to spell it out, but she was forced to. Laurel had to put a stop to this nonsense and clear the air—otherwise, it would destroy their marriage.

"I don't want her thinking there's a baby in our future," she continued. "You're going to build up her hopes, and there's never going to be a baby."

Her husband's mouth tightened, but he said nothing for several awkward seconds. He didn't need to; his look said everything. He didn't have the courage to speak out loud what his true feelings were. He wanted to keep believing, to cling to the possibility, even if it was a remote one.

Laurel could see the defiance in his eyes.

"Come on, Zach, we agreed on this. Children are simply not happening for us. They never will. We have to accept it and move forward."

Zach briefly closed his eyes. "I don't want to argue, especially when this isn't about us. It's about Nana."

"You're right," Laurel reluctantly agreed. "It's not about us. It's about Nana." She couldn't help worrying about her grandmother's unusual revelations about Mrs. Miracle, though. This angel-visitation stuff was something one would hear in Sunday school—not today in the here and now.

"Look at the difference Mrs. Miracle has already made," Zach reminded her. "Your grandmother's eyes are bright again. Her heart is full of hope. It's clear that this Mrs. Miracle, whoever and whatever she is, is good for Nana. Let's focus on that fact and let her believe what she wants. Let's enjoy seeing

Nana so full of life again, and more like her old self."

Her husband was right. She loved seeing her grandmother so happy and revitalized. Laurel didn't want to ruin Nana's newfound enjoyment. But Laurel wasn't about to let herself get wrapped up in this fantasy world.

"And if, by some miracle, a baby should happen to—"

"Zach, stop," Laurel pleaded. "Just stop. You know as well as I do this is a closed subject. Dead. Buried. Grieved."

"Oh, baby," Zach begged. "You know I would never intentionally hurt you, not after everything we've been through. All I'm asking is that you leave the door open just a crack."

Laurel stepped away from her husband and raised both hands, warning him off. "I can't . . . not after three expensive and grueling IVF treatments. Not after Jonathan. Do you seriously want us to go through that kind of heartache again? Is that what you want?"

With everything in her, she couldn't buy into it. Not again. Not when she'd been emotionally and physically depleted in their quest for a family. Only those who had suffered through infertility understood the desperation they faced as they waited for a baby, then the pain that came when they were denied at every turn.

Laurel's heart ached to watch her nana knit booties for a child she'd never hold or have the opportunity to love. Of course, once they were finished, if they ever were, she could always add them to the pile of newborn clothing to donate.

The following afternoon, Zach sat in his office cubicle, his hand on his phone and his mind working at warp speed. Laurel didn't know what he'd done. She didn't have a clue that a month after Jonathan had been claimed by his birth father, Zach had reached out to the adoption agency and asked that their names be reinstated. Guilt ate at him. He didn't want to think what Laurel would do if she ever found out. He hated keeping secrets from her, but it was better that she not know what he'd done. Nevertheless, it felt deceitful and dishonest on his part. Not telling her ate at him. His real fear was this: If he didn't tell Laurel, eventually the underhandedness of what he'd done would crumble the very foundation of their marriage.

Sucking in a breath, Zach punched in the number that would connect him to the adoption agency.

"Loving Families Adoption Services," the receptionist answered. "How may I direct your call?"

"May I speak with Mary Swindoll? This is Zach McCullough." Mary was the caseworker who had been assigned to them when they'd first applied for adoption.

No more than a moment later, Mary was on the line. "Zach. How good to hear your voice."

"Yours, too, Mary." The hollow chattiness was all Zach needed to hear to know there were no changes in their status, but he asked anyway. "I'm calling hoping for an update."

"I'm sorry, Zach. I know it's been a long time. Several babies have come up for adoption, and one specifically that we considered for you and Laurel, but something told me that the mother might have a change of heart. My instincts were right—she did pull out of the adoption right after the baby was born."

Zach was relieved that Mary was insightful, so they wouldn't have had their hopes set on that baby. Another incident like Jonathan would have destroyed his wife. Laurel might not have survived it. The truth was, Zach wasn't sure he could have, either. The first failed adoption had been hard enough.

"I appreciate your wisdom."

"I'll be in touch after the first of the year," Mary promised.

"Sure. Thanks for taking my call," Zach said, his words lacking emotion. As soon as he ended the call, a heavy sense of defeat fell upon his shoulders.

Laurel's day had been going along well. Although her students were already keyed up about Christmas and a visit from Santa, she had no trouble controlling her classroom. That didn't mean she wasn't ready for her break for lunch. Her stomach was growling.

The lounge was buzzing when Laurel entered. Spirits were high. One would think this was the last day of school before the winter break. Opening the refrigerator, she pulled out her roast beef sandwich and a bag of grapes. The roast from last night's dinner had been the best she'd ever tasted, and both she and Zach had used it to make sandwiches to bring to work.

Chase Walter pulled out a chair and sat down next to Laurel. "Did you hear the news?"

Almost immediately the room went eerily quiet.

"Chase," said Mona, who taught the other first-grade class. She glared at the fifth-grade teacher.

"What?" Chase demanded, glancing around the room, not understanding what he'd done that was so terrible.

"No, I hadn't. What news?" After her argument with Zach from the night before, Laurel was ready to hear something fun. Whatever the news was, it had the teachers' lounge humming with excitement.

"It's about me," replied Britta Jackson, who was another teacher.

Laurel liked Britta. Everyone did. She was a favorite not only with the staff, but also with the students and their parents. She had two children, one in junior high, and the other was a freshman in high school.

"Well, tell me," Laurel said, encouraging her friend to share.

The room went silent again, like everyone was waiting for a bombshell to drop.

"It's completely unexpected . . . I mean, it's almost a joke." Her friend was clearly nervous.

"What is?" Laurel asked.

"Wade, my husband, didn't even know what to

think. It took us some time to let it sink in that this could happen at our age."

"What happened?" Laurel pressed, not understanding the worried looks of her coworkers.

"I'm pregnant," Britta said, not meeting Laurel's eyes. "I never thought I'd be having a baby at my age."

Laurel's heart felt like it had stopped beating. Somehow, from some internal strength, she was able to dredge up a smile. "Congratulations, Britta. That's wonderful news."

CHAPTER FOUR

Mrs. Miracle arrived ten minutes before Laurel left for school the following day. Helen watched as her granddaughter pulled the caretaker aside. She could hear the two whispering in the kitchen and smiled to herself. She might be losing her memory and becoming more forgetful, but Helen was bright enough to know the subject of their conversation.

The whispering was sure to be about Helen's claim that Mrs. Miracle was an authentic, genuine angel. Laurel looked guilty after the talk, avoiding eye contact with her grandmother as she rushed out the door, making an excuse that she was running late for school.

Mrs. Miracle joined Helen, taking a seat on the sofa. She brought out her knitting.

Reaching for her own pair of knitting needles, Helen said, "They didn't believe me."

"I didn't expect they would, and neither should you."

Helen wished her granddaughter would have been more trusting. Then again, after the events of the last eighteen months, she couldn't really blame Laurel.

"She thinks I'm losing even more of my mind, doesn't she?"

Mrs. Miracle contemplated her reply as she wove the yarn through her fingers with the expertise of an accomplished knitter. "She is concerned, but that's only natural." She paused, resting the needles on her lap. "If anyone should be blamed for this, it falls squarely on me. It would've been better if I'd kept it a secret, as I often do. But by sharing it with you, and you passing it along to Laurel, it confirmed to her that your mental capabilities are failing at an increasing speed. That's far from the truth, as you and I both know."

"I should've been quiet about it," Helen said, regretting the impulse. If only she had thought matters through more carefully. "Are you upset with me? Was I wrong to tell them?" Helen hoped she hadn't alienated this angel who had come into her life, this caregiver whose companionship she'd come to treasure in such a short time.

"Not at all," Mrs. Miracle reassured her.

"You didn't tell me not to tell anyone. If you had, I would've kept the secret to myself."

"It's fine, Helen. Your granddaughter's faith is fragile at best. I've come for her and for Zach as much as I have for you." Finishing her row, she set the knitting on her lap. "It's such a lovely day. Do you feel up for a walk a bit later? It will do your heart good and take your thoughts off Laurel."

A walk was the perfect way to break Helen's melancholy mood, and she quickly agreed. The rain of the last few days had stopped, and the weather forecast was for intermittent clouds and sunshine. Helen welcomed the opportunity to breathe in the fresh air. Getting lost and confused in her own neighborhood had badly shaken her. Since that fateful day, she hadn't traveled outside for more than to collect the mail.

The two women knitted side by side for the next hour, chatting now and again, with the television keeping them company. Without asking, Mrs. Miracle turned the channel to the morning game show that Helen routinely enjoyed. She found it entertaining to watch the crazy things people were willing to do in order to participate in these silly games.

When the sun finally peeked out of the clouds and through the living room window, Mrs. Miracle stood and gathered their coats and scarves. "Let's venture out while we have sunshine."

"That would be lovely."

As they readied for their walk, Helen noticed the colorful Fair Isle scarf her home companion had around the collar of her gray wool coat. "Did you knit that scarf yourself?" she asked Mrs. Miracle as she put on her own coat and scarf.

"I did."

"It's lovely." Helen was impressed. She'd been

right to assume the other woman was an accomplished knitter.

Once outside, the two women looped their arms together and set off down the sidewalk. As they strolled together, Helen gave a detailed description of the family who had once occupied each house. All but one family had since moved. She dearly missed her old neighborhood friends. New families had moved in and Helen was unfamiliar with them. Most were young with small children.

"I don't know my new neighbors as well as I did my old ones. A few seem to know who I am, but I forget their names." She reluctantly admitted how she referred to them as "dear" or some other generic title whenever she'd bump into them.

Mrs. Miracle patted her hand, silently telling her she understood. It was a comforting gesture that encouraged Helen to continue sharing.

"The neighborhood has changed," she said, retelling her memories of when children once crowded the yards and sidewalks up and down the street. This was before video games, cellphones, and social media. "Children played outdoors, rode their bicycles, and had impromptu soccer games right in the middle of the street. I rarely see children outside these days."

Helen continued her reminiscing. "Robert and I always decorated the house for Christmas, as did most of the neighborhood. Only a few put up outdoor lights or displays anymore." One house had a family of lighted deer in the front yard. Another, five houses down, displayed a giant blown-up snowman.

"Christmas has always been my favorite holiday," Mrs. Miracle commented as they continued ambling down the sidewalk.

"I love Christmas, too," Helen reflected. She grew somber thinking back on the Christmases from long ago when Robert had been alive. Even now, seven years after his passing, she missed him. Not a day passed when he wasn't on her mind or in her heart. Sometimes she'd forget that he was gone. On those days, it was easier to pretend he was still alive. Occasionally, when no one was in the house, she'd carry on one-sided conversations with her late husband, out loud, pretending that he was there to listen to her ramblings.

One time, Laurel had overheard her talking to him and had grown worried. Laurel had taken Helen by the hand and gently let her know that Robert had died several years ago. Helen hadn't tried to explain herself and let it drop.

"You miss Robert, don't you?"

This angel seemed to be able to read her every thought. "Oh yes, so much. He was my everything."

"He misses you, too."

Helen's pulse accelerated upon hearing the news. "You've talked to Robert? In heaven?" Keeping her voice level was impossible. Excitement fizzed up inside her like a shaken soda.

"Of course. Meeting your family was part of my preparation for this assignment. I talked to your parents, your brother, your husband, and your daughter."

"You met my *Kelly*?" Her heart pounded so loud that it left a ringing noise in her ears.

"She's very much like you."

Tears gathered in Helen's eyes. Losing their daughter at such a young age had nearly destroyed them. Helen had leaned into God, but it had taken Robert time to let go of his grief and accept their daughter's untimely death.

Having Laurel come live with them had been a tremendous help in their recovery from losing their only child. Their full focus was now on the needs of a ten-year-old girl whose entire life had been turned upside down in the blink of an eye. When she'd arrived at their home, she'd been angry and confused. Laurel had not only lost her mother, her home, her friends, and her school, but all that was comfortable and familiar.

Michael, Laurel's father, had tried several live-in nannies to help with Laurel's care as his job required so much travel, but all those attempts had failed. After a lot of prayer, wisdom, and careful planning, Laurel's father sent her to live with her grandparents. It was exactly what everyone needed. Helen wrapped Laurel in arms of love and gave her the attention she so desperately longed for, while Robert gave the hurting young girl a sense of security. Michael visited often, which helped Laurel with the grieving process. Slowly, she began to thrive under her grandparents' care.

After Michael remarried, Laurel spent the summers with him and his new family. For a long time, Helen felt certain her granddaughter would want to return to live with him. It surprised and pleased her that Laurel chose to remain with them. The child had endured enough change in her short life, and starting over again at a different school and having to make new friends was more than Laurel could handle as a young teen.

Mrs. Miracle interrupted her thoughts. "Kelly works in the nursery in heaven. She loves the newborns best."

"She always did love babies," Helen remembered. Her daughter had longed for a large family and was able to carry only Laurel to full term, after several miscarriages. Like Helen, Kelly had only one child.

"Those babies love her. You'll see it all for yourself one day."

"One day," Helen repeated. She wondered how long it would be before she would join Robert and Kelly. Asking didn't seem right. She accepted the future was hidden for a reason. Helen was grateful not to have the ability to look ahead. If she had known in advance about losing both Kelly and Robert, it would have destroyed the precious time they'd had together on earth.

"Oh my," Helen exclaimed. "I'm doing it again. My mind wanders off, and I have no idea where I am. Where are we?" Looking around her, she stopped. Just like before, she didn't recognize where she was. If asked, she wouldn't know how to find her way back to the house.

"Don't worry, Helen. That's why I'm here. We're at the spot where you got lost when you chased after the loose puppy," Mrs. Miracle said.

Looking around, Helen didn't see anything that looked familiar. If her memory served her right, there used to be a church on this very corner. Next to it was a small park, or so she recalled. The park had vanished, as well as the church. Both had been replaced by a large condo building.

"Where's the church?" she asked, certain that it was on this very corner not long ago.

"It was torn down a couple years ago," Mrs. Miracle explained.

"Torn down?" That didn't seem right. Laurel had attended Vacation Bible School at that church the first year she'd come to live with Helen and Robert.

"It's sad, I agree. The property became valuable and the church couldn't afford to maintain the building any longer. They've moved to a new location."

"So many changes," Helen said, shaking her head. And it all happened so quickly. One day there was a church and playground for children, and in the blink of an eye, both were gone.

"Are you ready to head home?" Mrs. Miracle asked.

The wind had picked up, and the sun slid behind a dark cloud, bringing a chill to the air. "I suppose we should," she said, although she'd enjoyed the walk and the conversation.

They started back to the house in silence for a few minutes, when Helen interrupted.

"Would you tell me something about yourself?"

"Me?" Mrs. Miracle seemed surprised by the question.

"Please. Seeing that you know everything there is to know about me and my family, it's only fair that you tell me your own story . . . if that's allowed, that is."

"You're right, it isn't fair," she said with a chuckle. "First off, my name isn't technically Mrs. Miracle. I was given the name Merkel. On my first assignment here on earth, I was a nanny to two mischievous boys who couldn't properly pronounce my name. They called me Mrs. Miracle and I've gone by that ever since."

"Do you visit earth often?"

"Every now and again. I come as needed."

They continued walking, and Helen had so many questions she wanted to ask. She was unsure which one to ask first. "Can you tell me about heaven . . . what it's like?"

"Oh my. That's a difficult question." The other woman hesitated, unsure where to start.

"Is it anything like earth?"

"Yes . . . and no. There's beauty in heaven that can't be explained in words."

"You mentioned Kelly working in the nursery. If you must know, and it's a bit embarrassing to admit . . . I've always thought that the time we will spend in heaven will be like a really long church service."

Mrs. Miracle laughed. "I'm afraid far too many people believe that. You're right in assuming there's time to worship, but not twenty-four/seven. Speaking of time, there's no need for clocks, as time has no meaning."

" 'No meaning'?"

"That's something else that's hard to explain. It's eternity, with no beginning and no end. We aren't bound to the scientific laws of earth."

Helen took a moment to mull that over, wondering at the changes she would find in the afterlife. "Is there anything else you can tell me?"

"Oh, much more, but I don't want to overload you with details. You'll experience it yourself in due course, and then you'll be granted full understanding."

Helen wanted to know more about heaven. Death had never worried her. She knew it was coming, especially for a woman of her age. Dwelling on it was unproductive, and she had looked forward to her reunion with her family and friends when the time came.

"I *will* tell you that everyone in heaven is able to make use of the talents that God has given them."

"You mean we will all have jobs?"

She laughed at Helen's comment. "Not work, as you think of it on earth. We each have certain gifts given us. While on earth, we hold jobs. In heaven, our talents are maximized beyond a traditional workplace, bringing ourselves and others joy."

This was an entirely new concept to Helen. Until meeting Mrs. Miracle, Helen had never given heaven much thought. Now she continually thought about all the wonderful possibilities.

They continued back home and had just finished hanging up their coats when the house phone rang.

"Would you like me to answer that? It's Laurel," Mrs. Miracle told her, without having to look at the caller ID.

Grateful to know it wasn't another solicitation call, Helen nodded and picked up her knitting project.

"Hello," Mrs. Miracle greeted Laurel. She listened, then replied to Laurel's question.

"Yes, Laurel, Helen and I have had a good heart-to-heart, so you don't need to worry, dear."

The home companion spoke for a few minutes longer before she ended the call.

"Laurel is concerned about me, isn't she?"

"She is," Mrs. Miracle said. "I assured her you're doing well, and she's at ease now."

"Thank you. Laurel has a right to worry. I do get overly forgetful at times." She paused her knitting and sighed. "I forgot I'd put a load of laundry in the washer last week and it stayed there for two full days before I remembered."

"Laurel mentioned that."

Helen could well imagine all her granddaughter had to say about her shortcomings and her memory issues, but she knew her granddaughter did it out of love. Sometimes Helen was afraid to help around the house for fear she'd do something wrong and cause her granddaughter extra work instead. Feeling useless had a discomfort all on its own.

Mrs. Miracle gave Helen's hand a gentle squeeze. "It's fine, dear. You are surrounded by two people who care—they love you deeply. Neither Zach nor Laurel fault you. After all, if it wasn't for your forgetfulness, I wouldn't be here."

Her words brought a sense of relief and a smile to Helen.

"Are you ready for lunch?"

Helen often skipped meals while her granddaughter was at school. Then she recognized she hadn't had breakfast that morning. Or had she?

"Yes, let's make lunch," Helen said, rather than worry whether she had had breakfast or not. Her body told her she was hungry and that was answer enough.

Mrs. Miracle went about assembling their meal. She paused and a slow smile came over her. "You were asking me about heaven."

"Yes."

"Helen, one of the most amazing things about heaven is the food. The chefs are brilliant and there are delicious vegetables and fruits that eyes here on earth have never seen. Every day is a feast."

Helen's eyes widened, imagining what culinary delights awaited her.

"And the best part," Mrs. Miracle said with a twinkle in her eyes, "is that there isn't a scale in sight."

Laurel never fully understood what it was about the experience that had helped to change her outlook. Perhaps working closely by Nana's side as she rolled and cut out the dough, or maybe it was the joy she felt giving the cookies away. The tradition of baking gingerbread cutouts and other cookies, and then sharing them with others at Christmas, had continued to this day.

Zach arrived home. "Look outside," he called as he walked in the door, removing the moisture from his coat. "It's starting to snow."

"Snow?" Laurel hurried to the window. Sure enough, big, fat flakes lazily drifted from the sky, sparkling in the light like diamonds, then landing on the grass and quickly disappearing. Seeing the snowflakes and smelling the gingerbread cookies filled Laurel's heart with a burst of Christmas spirit, but she couldn't let go of the conversation from the night before. If she could only focus on Christmas, it would help. Laurel loved her husband and admired his determination and tenacity in most everything. But not in this. Not in his resolve to keep an open mind and believe that—out of the blue—a baby would miraculously appear on their doorstep. Their talk had deeply troubled her. If Zach wanted to keep believing and hold on to the hope of a child, she was afraid it would end badly for them.

"We need to get our Christmas tree," Laurel announced, trying to distract herself from that awful thought. "We can shop for it tonight, set it up, and decorate it together." Christmases with Zach had become her favorite time of the year. They did everything together—buying the tree, decorating it, shopping for gifts, baking—all while sharing the joy of the season.

Zach nodded, looking excited, until he looked over to Helen and the home companion. "We could go out, but it's time for Mrs. Miracle to head home, isn't it?" It went without saying that leaving Nana would be problematic. It was nearing the time of day when Helen often became even more confused and sometimes irritable.

The happy expectation Laurel felt moments earlier instantly faded. She was aware they couldn't leave her grandmother alone, and Mrs. Miracle had already put in a full eight hours. No doubt the caregiver was anxious to head back to her own home.

"Did someone mention getting a Christmas tree?" Mrs. Miracle asked, coming out of the kitchen to join Laurel and Zach in the living room.

"We'll wait for the weekend," Laurel said, as Zach started to remove his coat.

"Nonsense," Mrs. Miracle said. "You two go ahead. Go pick up your tree, and while you're out, take time to have dinner—just the two of you. Every couple needs a date night now and then. Helen and I are having a grand time."

"But you've already put in a full day and—"

"If you're worried about the overtime, then don't. The agency has a holiday special which allows for exactly this sort of thing. All through December, it's a flat fee, no matter how many hours I spend here with Helen."

"I don't recall hearing that from the woman I spoke with," Laurel said.

"She probably didn't tell you when you first called, because she didn't think a Caring Angel would be available for your grandmother until after the first of the year."

Zach looked to Laurel to make the decision. It'd been weeks since they'd enjoyed a night out. Date night had become a thing of the past since Helen's dementia had become substantially worse.

"You're sure you're able to stay?"

"Heavens, yes. Now head out and enjoy yourself. Find the perfect Christmas tree."

Expressing their thanks, Zach reached for Laurel's hand, her coat, and her gloves, and rushed her out of the house, not wanting Mrs. Miracle to change her mind.

"Hey," Laurel said and laughed, attempting to put her coat on as they headed to the car. "Give me a second," she said, giggling like one of her students, excited and happy. The snow had continued to fall, and she paused and held out her arms, catching a few of the fat flakes in the palms of her hands.

"Where should we go first?" Zach asked. "Dinner, or the tree?"

"Tree shopping," Laurel said, giddy with happiness. "Then to dinner."

"Perfect."

Wrapping her arm around his elbow, Zach walked her to his car and opened the passenger door for her. Leaning in, he soundly kissed her, leaving her dizzy with longing and warmth. It was like the old days, when they were first married, when it felt like nothing could ever go wrong. More than any-thing, Laurel wanted to enjoy this night without the tension she'd felt from the night before. She placed her hands on each side of Zach's head and kissed him back.

"I can't think of the last time we went out—just the two of us," Zach said, climbing behind the wheel and starting the engine.

Sad as it was to say, neither could Laurel. Even after they'd moved in with Nana, their tight budget, due to paying back the bills for fertility treatments, hadn't been flexible enough to include entertain-ment. Date night consisted of a television movie with a frozen pizza. And then her grandmother's mental health began to decline, which limited their ability to get out in the evenings.

"I want a big tree this year," Laurel said as they headed to the neighborhood tree lot.

"You got it."

As Zach drove around Lake Union past Gas Works Park, he reached for Laurel's hand. "Do you recall when we were first dating—how we used to lie out on the grass in the middle of summer and gaze into the heavens?"

It wasn't like Laurel would forget. Those were nights when they'd shared their hopes and dreams for the future—special times that had made them grow closer. It was the following autumn that Zach had asked her to be his wife.

"We talked about everything," Laurel recalled. "Our future seemed bright. Me as a teacher, and you doing amazingly great and geeky computer programming for Amazon. Nothing could stand in our way."

"We were going to build our own home, design it ourselves, or remodel an existing one. I wanted to live on Capitol Hill, and you were set on Ballard. A four-bedroom house with a den for you. Two kids and at least one dog, right?"

"Two children," she repeated slowly. "Was that to remind me how I have failed you as a wife?"

"No," Zach nearly shouted. "No, never. How can you even suggest such a thing?"

"I can't give you children," Laurel bitterly replied. It hurt to whisper the words. She felt like a failure, a disappointment to the man she loved. Yet through it all, Zach had faithfully remained at her side. Not once had he complained or spoken of his own sense of loss. He'd been the one to hold her together after Jonathan was taken from them. During the IVF attempts he'd been there for her, encouraging and supporting her while her body underwent hormone treatments, painful shots, and repeated failures. And when she'd failed to conceive, he'd held her while she'd wept with disappointment.

"You've given me so much more than children, Laurel. I'm sorry, forgive me. I know how painful this is for you . . . It's just that I was thinking about those nights. I didn't mean anything by it."

Laurel didn't want to do or say anything that would put a damper on their evening out, so she kept quiet. Maybe she was being oversensitive, but she couldn't help feeling like she'd let her husband down.

"Let's enjoy tonight. We don't get many of these anymore," he said.

"You're right. No more talk about things that weren't meant to be. This evening is about the here and now. About us."

They stopped at the lot selling trees and Laurel must have looked at two dozen, making Zach stand each one up so she could get the full view. She marveled at her husband's patience as he stamped each tree on the ground several times and held it for her inspection, until she found the perfect one. It was full, freshly cut, and it smelled of pine and of Christmas—the way the trees were from her early childhood, from the precious times she'd chosen them with her mom and dad.

Zach paid for the tree, and one of the teens from the scout troop helped him mount it on the roof of his car.

"I don't know about you, but I could use something to chase away the chill," Zach said.

Starbucks was directly across from the lot, and they headed in that direction. Within a few minutes, they each had a hot drink in their hands and had found a small table where they could sit and talk. Laurel's thoughts went to Christmases past.

"The year before my mom died, she and I made our own ornaments. Dad mailed them to Nana the first Christmas after I went to live with them. They were ugly—especially the ones I made—but to me, they were perfect."

"Beauty is in the eye of the beholder, right?"

"We used molds and filled them with plaster of paris, then painted them. Nana and I placed them on the tree every year until they finally had all crumbled into chunks." Laurel hadn't thought about those ornaments in years. How she wished she could put her hands on one of them again. To see one, to touch one—it would be a small way of having her mother with her again at Christmas. Memories of that final Christmas with her mother warmed Laurel as much or more than the peppermint latte in her hands.

"An old ornament like that I could have used for the white-elephant exchange at work again this year," Zach mentioned, looking comfortable and relaxed, leaning back against his chair. "Any idea what I can bring?"

Zach had no idea what the plaster-of-paris ornament meant to her.

Rather than explain, she said, "What about that horrible gray sweater you got last year with the pink polka dots?"

"Hey—I like that sweater!" Zach teased.

"Sure you do. And how many times have you worn it?"

"Never," he said, cringing at the thought. "Putting it back in the exchange is the perfect way to be rid of it."

Drinking the last of her latte, she tossed her cup into the garbage.

"You ready for dinner?" Zach asked, discarding his own cup.

"Sure. What are you in the mood for?"

"Food."

"How about Mexican?" Laurel knew that was Zach's go-to favorite, and it was also one of her own.

"There's a place on the waterfront that I've been wanting to try. We could leave the car here and hop on the bus over. You up for that?"

That sounded perfect to Laurel. She loved walking along the Seattle waterfront at night, with the trees along the street glowing with white lights and the fully lit ferryboats steering through the dark waters of Puget Sound. The Ferris wheel's huge orb illuminated the sky, while the salty scent coming from the water hung in the air.

"I'll ask the attendant if he can keep an eye on the tree for us," Zach said. They walked back to the tree lot and Zach spoke to the teen, who readily agreed to look after their car and tree if they returned before ten when the lot closed.

A city bus pulled up within minutes and they hopped on, quickly finding seats. They rode through the busy downtown streets until they reached the waterfront. Stepping off the bus, Laurel paused and closed her eyes, taking in the smells of the night. The aroma of steamed clams, oysters, salmon, and clam chowder from the nearby restaurants filled the air.

Zach led her to the Mexican restaurant, which had dozens of artificial poinsettias lining the dock railing. The outside seating area was closed for the winter. In summer, there was always a waiting list for outside dining.

"I've walked past Moctezuma's dozens of times and it always seems to be busy, so I have to assume the food is good," Zach commented.

Because it was almost seven-thirty by the time they'd arrived, they were seated right away. The menu, along with a bowl of chips and salsa, was immediately delivered to the table. The chips were hot and salty, exactly the way she liked them.

Zach always ordered the same thing—enchiladas—so he barely perused the menu. Laurel took her time, bouncing from one page to the next, reading the details of each dish, until she finally decided on the tortilla soup.

They were served within a few minutes and ate and talked, each having a margarita. They lingered at the table with their earlier, painful conversation put behind them. The evening was perfect until Laurel noticed that Zach was avoiding eye contact. She wondered if there was something bothering him. Something he was reluctant to mention.

"Zach? Is everything all right?"

"Of course. What makes you ask?" He sounded almost defensive.

"You're looking pensive, like there's something you want to tell me."

He quickly denied it. "Everything is perfect. How could it not be?"

Appearing to change the subject intentionally, Zach glanced at the time. "It's late. We need to get back."

Laurel couldn't believe it was already after nine. The time had gone by so quickly. Zach paid for the meal, and they got on the first bus heading back in the direction of the tree lot. Their hearts racing, they returned to their vehicle, breathless. The scoutmaster was just closing for the night.

"I feel awful staying out this late," Laurel said to Zach on the drive home, convinced that Mrs. Miracle would think they'd taken advantage of her generous offer.

"I do, too. I have no idea where the time went."

Laurel was surprised to see the living room lights on when Zach pulled the car into the driveway. While he untied the tree from the roof of the car, she hurried into the house to find Mrs. Miracle sitting in front of the television, knitting in her hands, looking calm and content.

"I am so sorry," Laurel blurted out. "Zach and I . . . The time flew by. We had no idea it was this late."

"Don't you fret," Mrs. Miracle said, dismissing her apology with a sweep of her hand. "I've had a relaxing evening. Your grandmother and I stayed up and talked. She went to bed less than thirty minutes ago."

It was unusual for Nana to stay up so late.

"We lost track of time sharing stories. She may sleep late in the morning." The caregiver gathered her knitting bag and her coat. "I'll see you first thing in the morning."

"Are you sure? I mean . . . wouldn't you rather sleep in? I'm sure Nana will be fine by herself for a few hours. I'm certainly able to take a few hours of personal leave and stay with her until you arrive." Mrs. Miracle was older herself, and surely she'd need a good night of sleep after such a long day.

"Nonsense," Mrs. Miracle insisted. "I'll be here bright and early, the same as always."

As she was about to walk out the door, Zach appeared with the Christmas tree.

Mrs. Miracle stepped aside to let him pass into the living room. She paused to admire the tree. "It's perfect," she said.

"My wife has exquisite taste."

"Yes, she does," Mrs. Miracle agreed. And with that, she was out the door.

Although it wasn't an easy feat, Laurel and Zach managed to get the tree in the holder and added water. With both their busy work schedules, they knew that they wouldn't get around to decorating it until the weekend.

Early the next morning, Mrs. Miracle arrived on time, looking well rested and ready for a new day. Nana, as her home companion had predicted, remained in bed, sound asleep.

"You've got the tree up," Mrs. Miracle said, "and that's the perfect spot."

"It's where Gramps placed it every year. Unfortunately, we didn't have time to do anything more than set it up," Laurel said with a sigh. "We'll have to wait for the weekend to decorate it."

"Would you like your grandmother and me to do it?"

Laurel was taken aback by the offer. She hadn't meant to insinuate that Mrs. Miracle should take on such a big task. "Oh no. Please, you've already done so much. We'll find the time. I didn't mean to imply anything."

"You didn't. I offered. Reliving favorite times, such as decorating the tree, making cookies . . . bringing these to the forefront of your grandmother's mind might help her regain treasured memories that have been buried for some time now."

Laurel understood what the caregiver was telling her. Happy thoughts and good memories were what Nana needed. If Mrs. Miracle could budge those loose, it'd be good for her grandmother.

"Then by all means, give it a try," Laurel agreed. "We brought everything down from the attic before we went to bed."

"I believe we'll have a perfect day."

And Laurel believed it, too.

As Laurel's day progressed, she worried at the wisdom of her decision to let the two ladies decorate the tree. Her grandmother was in her late seventies, and Mrs. Miracle had to be in her mid-sixties, if not older. It was hard to tell. What had she been thinking? The tree, with its fullness and girth, not to mention its height, had been difficult for Laurel and Zach to get into the holder. And it would most certainly require the use of the stepladder they'd left out the night before. Adding lights to a tree would've been a challenge for her and Zach, let alone her grandmother and Mrs. Miracle. And putting an angel at the top? She shivered at the thought. At her lunch break, she sent Mrs. Miracle a text to check in, and within seconds she got a reply.

All is well. Never better.

Regardless of the reply, Laurel couldn't help being concerned.

The first thing Laurel saw upon pulling into the driveway later that afternoon was the brightly lit Christmas tree through the living room window. For half a second, she thought she had the wrong house. The tree looked like something out of a holiday movie. There must have been a thousand tiny lights on it. Even from the outside looking in, she could see that it was fully covered with a ridiculous amount of decorations in every size, shape, and color.

When she reached the front door, Nana greeted her. "What do you think?" she asked Laurel, her eyes bright and smiling. Tugging on Laurel's arm, she brought her granddaughter into the house, dragging her over to stand in front of the tree.

Laurel was afraid she looked like a bass out of water, mouth wide open, hardly able to take it all in. "It's . . . stunning."

"It's the most beautiful Christmas tree ever," Nana agreed, clapping her hands together.

"You two did all this yourself? You didn't hire elves to help you?"

"We did," Mrs. Miracle answered, winking at Laurel's grandmother.

"And, Laurel, look what we found." Nana pointed at an old, worn bell-shaped ornament—the very one that Laurel had made years ago with her mother.

"How . . . How is this possible?" she whispered, even as tears gathered in her eyes. "This ornament fell apart years ago. Just last night, I told Zach how I wished I'd been able to salvage at least one that Mom and I had made."

Both women looked at each other, then at her, and smiled.

"Mrs. Miracle found several other boxes in the garage," Nana said. "Your grandfather must have set it aside."

"I can't believe it." Laurel had been through that garage several times. She didn't recall her grandparents having more than a few storage tubs of Christmas decorations, all stored in the attic. She was certain she wouldn't have overlooked something so precious to her, even though to another's eyes, it had no value.

"Yet here it is," Nana said. "Aren't you pleased?"

"Oh yes." It was the season, after all, and this year, for sure. The season of miracles.

CHAPTER SIX

Laurel woke early the following morning and wandered from her and Zach's bedroom to the kitchen. She paused as she passed by the living room, instantly drawn to the Christmas tree and the sad-looking ornament that only a mother could love—the one that she'd crafted all those years ago. She had to practically look cross-eyed to reimagine its original bell shape. Tucked near the shiny glass ornaments and glittering lights, that handmade, battered plaster-of-paris bell with pink sparkles looked like it'd been made by the clumsy hands of a nine-year-old, which indeed it had been.

The craft and beauty of the tree was above and beyond anything she and Zach could have managed. This was more than a simple family tree, it was a work of art. Again, she marveled at how Mrs. Miracle and her grandmother had been able to pull it off.

Zach joined her for a quick moment, sipping his coffee before he headed out the door. They'd spent an extra ten minutes cuddling in bed after the alarm went off. For the last two nights, they'd made love late into the night, holding each other closely, neither speaking of the strange events taking place around them. Nana's remarkable improvements, the supposed angel in their home, the magical reappearance of that formerly lost and now found precious tree ornament. Laurel suspected something was going on with Zach, but she hadn't had the courage to confront him, not when she knew the answers might endanger their marriage.

Only those who had faced the same infertility issues as she had could relate to the doubts and feelings of inadequacy that she felt every day. Opening her own heart to even the possibility was beyond her. She couldn't bring herself to do it. She simply couldn't.

"I'm off to the coal mines," Zach said as he kissed her cheek. He'd be working late tonight and wouldn't be home until after dinner.

"Don't forget that I'll be home briefly after school, then I head back to meet with the parents who are helping with the holiday program." The December school production had been in the works for more than two months now. Several parents had volunteered to help. Before Laurel had agreed to oversee the production, she'd planned for her neighbor to stay with her grandmother when she had rehearsals. But now Mrs. Miracle was available and willing to extend her hours.

"We'll connect later then," her husband replied. "I'll probably get home before you."

"Have a good day."

"How can I *not* have a great day, after the night we shared?" he whispered back, for her ears alone.

Laurel blushed as she stood before the tree, unable to appreciate its beauty. It could be her insecurities, her imagination, but she sensed that Zach was trying too hard to convince her that all was well with him, to assure her that he'd reached the same acceptance she had.

Shaking these thoughts from her head, she looked at their Christmas tree again and was mesmerized at the sight. Nothing from her childhood compared with it. She'd admired the professionally decorated trees in all the downtown window displays, but this one put even those to shame. It was hard to believe that the two older women had managed this.

Mrs. Miracle had arrived and was already busy in the kitchen, getting breakfast ready for Nana. Laurel joined her and set her coffee mug in the sink.

"Were you an interior decorator in another life?" she asked Mrs. Miracle.

The older woman paused and looked over her shoulder, surprise showing in her eyes. "What makes you think that?"

"The Christmas tree. It's stunning. I've never seen anything like it, and trust me, I've seen a lot of showstopping trees. You must have had some sort of professional experience."

The older woman laughed, finding the comment amusing. "Me? A professional decorator? Never."

"Then you have an innate talent for it," Laurel concluded.

She was about to walk out the door when her grandmother appeared in the kitchen, dressed for the day and looking ten years younger. Laurel marveled at the new energy and spirit she'd noticed in her grandmother and wondered why it had taken her so long to recognize her grandmother's needs. Being home alone every day must have been depressing and lonely. Paying the monthly fee to have a Caring Angel was certainly going to be a challenge to their budget, but the benefits were worth every penny. The changes in her grandmother were nothing short of miraculous. Her observation produced a smile, seeing that the caregiver was indeed a Mrs. Miracle.

"Good morning, Laurel," Nana greeted her, hugging her granddaughter for an extra heartbeat.

"Did you sleep well, Nana?"

"Like a lazy kitten."

A picture formed in Laurel's head of a tiny cat curled up on a chair, snoozing without a care in the world.

"I had a wonderful dream," Nana continued.

"Was it about Gramps?"

"No," Nana replied. "It was about you."

"Me?"

"Yes. You, and Zach, and . . ." She paused, as if she had said more than she should.

Out of the corner of her eye, Laurel saw Mrs.

Miracle gently shake her head, seeming to tell Nana not to say anything more. The gesture seemed strange, and she would've inquired further if her grandmother hadn't continued to speak.

"The dream was about you and Zach," she repeated. "It was a good dream, a happy dream. It does my heart good to see you married to your best friend."

How right her nana was. Zach *was* her best friend, and rather than concentrating on what they didn't have, they needed to focus on what they did have—each other. They had so much to be grateful for, which was something she tended to forget in her pain and disappointments.

"You're right, Nana, so right." Laurel gently hugged her and then headed out the door, hurrying now because she was leaving the house later than she liked to.

Helen watched her granddaughter depart and wished she'd been able to explain her dream. Mrs. Miracle was right to stop her. Mentioning the dream and the baby that was due to arrive wouldn't have comforted Laurel, it would have done just the opposite. The dream had been lovely, and she'd held on to it as long as she could, wrapping her consciousness around the images, until it had faded from view like fog lifting from Puget Sound.

Mrs. Miracle joined her, and the two women stood together, peering out the window as Laurel climbed into her car and sped away. The Caring Angel gently touched Helen's arm.

"Laurel isn't ready yet. Telling her your dream would only have hurt her."

"I wish I could've shared it with her. It was such a vivid dream. I can't help but believe that it will all come to pass just the way it happened while I was asleep . . . just the way you told me it would."

"God often speaks to us in dreams, Helen."

Helen nodded. Robert had come to her in a dream a year after he'd died, almost to the day. Feeling sad and lonely, she'd gone to bed early and then found she couldn't sleep. After several hours of tossing and turning, she drifted into a semisleep, half awake and half asleep. Suddenly he was there with her, full of laughter and life, just as it had always been with the two of them, even after all the years of marriage.

"You're here," she'd said to him, although Helen wasn't sure if she'd said the words out loud or not.

Robert hadn't answered, although she'd desperately wanted him to speak.

"I miss you so much."

He'd grinned, letting her know he'd also missed her.

And then he was gone. Gone. Vanished, like he'd never been there in the room in the first place.

Helen had lain there, tears leaking from her eyes, so desperately wanting to call him back. At some point she must have drifted back into a deep sleep. When she woke the following morning, she was convinced she had somehow fabricated the entire episode. She reasoned this sort of thing didn't happen, that it had all been part of her grief and her imagination. She'd missed him and dreamed he'd come to her.

Suddenly, she rationalized that if Mrs. Miracle was an angel, the way she claimed to be, then certainly she would know the truth of that night.

"Robert came to me one night, didn't he?" she said, closely watching the other woman's expression, seeking any telltale sign.

"He did. It was his way of letting you know he was happy, and that he deeply loved you."

Helen blinked back tears. "I miss him, even now."

Mrs. Miracle's arm came around Helen. "I know you do. That's the price we pay when we love. It's joy and loss all wrapped up in one package. The thing you need to hold on to, and Laurel, too, is that while the heart may shatter into a thousand pieces, the soul remains intact."

Perhaps it was all the emotion that she felt at that moment, all this talk about Robert. Whatever it was, Helen suddenly felt terribly light-headed and needed to sit down. She feared if she didn't, she might collapse.

Mrs. Miracle gently and carefully guided Helen to her favorite chair without her having to ask for help.

"Let me get you some tea," the other woman said, disappearing into the kitchen. Helen could hear her bustling about, the click of the gas burner being turned on, the opening and closing of cupboard doors, and the kettle whistling.

Helen closed her eyes while she waited. Tea had been her dear mother's solution to nearly every problem. When James, her brother, had been in a fight at school, her mother had greeted her father at the door with a cup of tea upon his return from a long day in the fields. Only then did she break the news. Or if a bad grade at school deeply distressed her mother, the hot water was put on for tea. And when a neighbor stopped by to bemoan the loss of her husband's job? Doubly strong tea. Her mother once told her that every problem in life could be settled with three things: a hot cup of tea, enough time, and God's wisdom.

Mrs. Miracle returned shortly with the steaming tea, served in an antique china teacup that had belonged to Helen's mother.

"Drink this and rest. You'll feel better in a few minutes."

Helen did as she was told. The flavor was richer than anything she'd had before, but she didn't question the contents. In no time at all, it seemed, she was herself again, energized and ready to get on with her day. She suddenly felt the desire to venture out and explore the town, especially now that she had her own personal angel to escort her. It'd been a few years since she'd gone shopping with her granddaughter.

"How about doing a bit of Christmas shopping?" Helen suggested. "It's been so long since I've gone into town, and there's no better time than the present."

Mrs. Miracle smiled. "That's a wonderful idea."

They waited until mid-morning and then caught the bus to the downtown shopping district. The streets were filled with shoppers, the air festive with the sound of the bell-ringers. A vendor stood on the corner selling hot chestnuts, bringing back childhood memories for Helen. She paused, sure she could smell cinnamon blended in with the smell of freshly cut evergreens.

They walked arm in arm toward Pacific Place, the shopping mall in the heart of downtown Seattle. A group of carolers strolled past, dressed in Victorian costumes, complete with fur mufflers and long wool coats. The men wore top hats and knitted scarves. Helen and Mrs. Miracle paused to listen to the singers' harmonizing voices until they faded as they rounded the corner.

"This is everything that I remember about Christmas," Helen said, pausing to look inside the Nordstrom windows at the long line of parents with impatient children awaiting their turn to visit Santa.

Helen recalled taking Laurel here for her picture the first Christmas she'd come to live with them, despite the ten-year-old's protests that she was too old. The pictures that were returned to them in the mail spoke volumes of the grief lingering in Laurel's heart. Helen had been desperate, doing everything she could to bring a smile to that grieving child. Nothing had worked, until they'd baked those gingerbread men.

Stepping out of the cold, Helen and Mrs. Miracle walked into the mall and took the escalator to the second floor, to Laurel's favorite stationery store. Helen wanted to purchase a box of high-quality stationery for her granddaughter, knowing how much Laurel would treasure this gift.

As she was about to head to the cashier, Helen's eyes landed on a shelf displaying baby announcements. Glancing over her shoulder, she smiled at Mrs. Miracle. "It's a girl, you say?"

Mrs. Miracle grinned and nodded.

Helen added a box to the basket on her arm, knowing that Laurel would love to use her own beautiful handwriting for the exquisite announcements rather than spend money for the online version. "Should I put those under the tree? Or wait until after Christmas to give them to her?"

"The tree," Mrs. Miracle advised with a twinkle in her eye.

Helen's heart swelled. Laurel had to hold on only a while longer.

They ate lunch at a lovely Italian restaurant, both savoring the ravioli. Splurging, Helen enjoyed a glass of wine with their meal and felt light-headed again for an entirely different reason.

"You shouldn't have let me order that Chianti," she chastised her friend.

"No worries. I'll make sure we make it home safe and sound."

Once they finished lunch, Helen wanted to stroll down to Pike Place Market. She'd always loved the unique market, which happened to be the longest-running farmers' market in the States, a fact that all of Seattle was proud to boast.

As they walked past the shop that sold Beecher's

cheese, Helen noticed a line extending out the door for the original Starbucks. It amazed her to see so many willing to wait for the experience of paying five dollars for a cup of coffee. Several were looking at their phones, hardly aware of the moving line.

They stepped across the street and into the market. Pike Place Market was a wonderland of sights and sounds, of fishmongers tossing salmon, and of colorfully displayed fresh vegetables and fruits. Booth after booth of craftspeople were selling their wares, from leather goods to flavored honeys, spiced nuts, and beautifully arranged Christmas bouquets.

Mrs. Miracle paused long enough to look over the figurines crafted out of ash from the 1980 eruption of Mount Saint Helens. Thinking Zach might use the collectible as a paperweight on his work desk, Helen purchased one shaped like an orca, knowing how much he liked whales.

The crowds were thick and the two stayed only long enough to make their way through the upper floor. A walkway from the market led down to the waterfront, but by then Helen had grown tired, and they made their way by bus back to the house.

When Laurel returned from school, she found Helen sitting in her chair, knitting. "How was your day?" Helen asked her granddaughter.

"Busy. What about you?"

"Mrs. Miracle and I had a wonderful day," Helen said, sharing a satisfied smile with her Caring Angel.

CHAPTER SEVEN

Helen watched as Laurel left the house to return to school for the meeting with the parents regarding the holiday program. As soon as the door closed, Helen looked toward her companion.

"I want so badly to tell her about the baby that's coming," she said with a disgruntled sigh.

Mrs. Miracle joined her in the living room, delivering a fragrant cup of Christmas tea along with a plate of cookies. She sat next to Helen and gently patted her hand. "Now isn't the time, dear."

Helen trusted her angel friend. How could she not, seeing that Mrs. Miracle had been sent specifically for this mission? Her granddaughter was certain to think this news was yet another sign of Helen's dementia.

"She would pretend she didn't hear me, wouldn't she? She might even laugh it off," she said, knowing the subject of a baby was the last thing her grand-daughter would want to discuss.

"Sarah did, too, if you recall."

"Sarah?" Helen couldn't recall anyone in her ac-quaintance with that name.

"Yes, Abraham's Sarah. When the angel of the Lord came to Abraham and told him he would have a son at that time in the following year, Sarah over-heard and did her best to smother a laugh."

Ah yes, the Bible story. Helen knew it well. While Helen understood that her granddaughter might doubt her sanity, she wished there was a way she could infuse Laurel with faith. She badly wanted to give her granddaughter a reason to believe without outright announcing there would soon be an infant in her arms. She trusted that Mrs. Miracle knew best.

Her eyes returned to the Christmas tree. She was mesmerized by it, caught up in the memories of Christmas past. How quickly the years had flown by. It seemed like only yesterday that the troubled ten-year-old Laurel had come to live with her and Rob-ert. And here she was now, married and teaching at the local school, the very one her daughter, Kelly, had attended. As an adult, her granddaughter's heart was once again hurting, as she dealt with an-other significant loss. Only this time, baking cook-ies wasn't going to help smooth the road.

"Laurel has reached a place of resignation," her companion said. "That's understandable, but Zach isn't there yet. What I'm hoping is that Laurel will see all that's good in her life, instead of focusing on what she doesn't have, and be grateful for what she does."

Mrs. Miracle was right, Laurel needed to find a way to be genuinely grateful for what she had, not sorry for what she was lacking, and let that gratitude fill the hole in her heart.

Caught up in her musing, she hadn't noticed that her friend had left the room. It was several moments before Mrs. Miracle returned, carrying a dilapidated box with her.

"What in heaven's name is that?"

"I believe it's the nativity set you mentioned," she said. While on the bus ride home, Helen had reminisced about the set from her childhood that she'd once had and lost.

Helen's musings quickly came to a halt. "Where did you find it? Was it stored in the garage, like all those other long-lost ornaments you discovered?"

The other woman smiled and left the question unanswered. "Where would you like me to put it up?"

Her mother had set up the ceramic nativity scene every Christmas on a small table next to the fireplace in the family's farmhouse. It was the first thing visitors saw when entering their home during the Christmas season. It was the item she'd wanted most when her parents had passed. Over the years, several of the pieces had been broken. The original set had seventeen pieces but had dwindled down to three or four. Helen had despaired when the arm of the Baby Jesus had cracked. She glued the Christ Child back together as best she could, and tucked the remaining pieces away in Bubble Wrap, never pulling them out of storage after that.

"It's a lovely set."

"It was at one time," Helen agreed, saddened by the loss. "I made the mistake of placing it under the tree. Kelly loved the animals and would play with them. She was careful, but accidents happen. I should've known better than to let her treat them as toys, seeing how precious that set was to me. The donkey and one of the sheep were the first to be broken."

"Yes, children do love playing with nativity scene pieces."

Kelly had wept at the loss of that donkey, and she was genuinely sorry. Silent tears had fallen from Helen's eyes, too.

"What would you think if we put it up on the end table closest to the tree?" Mrs. Miracle asked.

That sounded fine with Helen. The tea had cooled, and she sipped it. The orange-cinnamon flavor was the perfect complement to the season and exactly what she needed after their shopping expedition.

While she relaxed, the caregiver disappeared for a few minutes and returned with a second box. She set it down and carefully unwrapped each piece of Helen's long-lost nativity set.

All seventeen pieces.

Watching in astonishment, Helen closed her eyes and smiled. Why was she shocked? Mrs. Miracle had made no secret of her heavenly connection.

This was simply one more fun surprise. One more miracle.

Mrs. Miracle placed the baby in the manger in the center of the table before she added two more of the figurines: Mary and Joseph. The shepherds appeared next, along with a variety of barnyard animals. The last to be set into place were the host of heavenly angels.

"The angels were always my favorite," Helen said, caught up in the memories of Christmas as a child.

"Were they?" Mrs. Miracle asked, seemingly delighted. "Several of my closest friends were in the countryside of Bethlehem that very night."

Helen waited, certain there was a story to be told.

"Shirley couldn't stay away. She isn't one of the Caring Angels here on earth like me."

"She isn't?" Helen asked, genuinely interested. "And Shirley? Angels have human names?"

"Yes. Shirley is part of a trio of angels who are my dearest friends."

"Are they guardian angels?"

"No, my friends are classified as prayer ambassadors."

Helen was unfamiliar with the term. "What's the difference between what you do and what they do?"

"Let me explain. Gabriel assigns the ambassador angels to answer prayers, which doesn't require taking on human form. As a Caring Angel, I'm able to do that as needed."

"So prayer ambassador angels aren't able to appear as humans . . . like you or me?"

"Not unless it's absolutely necessary, although my friends have pushed the limits of that rule on several occasions."

Helen could see that the Caring Angel was having trouble holding back a smile. "Oh?"

"Answering prayers isn't as easy as it sounds," Mrs. Miracle clarified, growing serious once again. "First off, Goodness and Mercy tend to be somewhat free-spirited. No pun intended. They are intrigued by earth and its people. All too often, they manage to get caught up in the lives of those they've been assigned to help, only to forget the original reason they've been given their assignment."

"Can you give me an example of what you mean?" Helen had been listening intently but wasn't sure she fully understood.

"Well . . ." Mrs. Miracle hesitated and looked over her shoulder, in case someone might be listening in on their conversation. "You see, the role of prayer ambassadors is more than answering prayers. Before they can complete their mission, their end goal is to teach a lesson to the human assigned to them."

"What kind of lesson?" Helen leaned forward to better hear the explanation. This business about the angels' duties intrigued her.

Tapping her finger against her lower lip, Mrs. Miracle appeared deep in thought. "This isn't my area of expertise, you understand."

"But you know more than you're saying."

"I do," she agreed, "but I'm not free to share any more information than I already have."

That made sense.

"I can tell you this much," the other woman continued. "Once the prayer is recorded, Gabriel reads it over and assigns it to the most qualified angel to find the answer. The key element for each angel is to be certain to teach the one who prays what they need to learn. Rest assured, every prayer is answered in God's time."

"Every prayer?"

"Oh yes, but not always the way one might want or expect. God knows best, and humans are left to accept that on faith."

"What were the names of your friends again?"

"Shirley, Goodness, and Mercy."

Helen leaned her head back, closed her eyes, and smiled. " 'Surely goodness and mercy will follow me all the days of my life,' " she quoted. "Like the Twenty-third Psalm?"

"That's right."

"And you say these three angels are your dearest friends?"

"They are," she confirmed. "And when the time comes, and you're called to heaven, you'll meet them yourself."

"I'll look forward to it." Helen's mental abilities might not be what they once were, and her body was slowly giving out, but that was to be expected. She still had time yet and was feeling like her much younger self since her companion's arrival.

"Getting back to that first Christmas," Mrs.

Miracle continued, "Shirley, Goodness, and Mercy were there with the heavenly host of angels who visited the shepherds—they were far too excited to stay away. Unfortunately, Shirley sang off-key, but the shepherds didn't appear to notice."

Helen laughed. "I'm not musically inclined myself, so she and I suffer the same problem."

"Shirley volunteered to stay behind to watch over the flocks while the shepherds hurried into the city to see the baby the angels told them about."

"Poor Shirley."

"Goodness and Mercy both stayed behind to help. There were plenty of angels that night at the manger to help celebrate, so they weren't missed, especially since they had already crashed the party on the hillside."

"What a glorious night that must have been! Do you see your friends often?"

"Not nearly as often as I'd like."

The nativity scene was in place now, and Mrs. Miracle stepped aside so Helen could view it. "What do you think?"

"It's exactly like it used to be," Helen said, thinking back to her childhood when her mother had arranged the pieces. They were in the same position as her mother had placed them all those years ago.

"Tell me more about the angels," Helen said, wanting to learn everything she could.

"I dare not. I shouldn't have said as much as I already did. It would be far too easy for you to forget in the excitement of the season and repeat what I said to Laurel and Zach."

"Oh dear, you're right. I should have never mentioned you're an angel. I'm so sorry."

"No worries, dear one," Mrs. Miracle assured her. "My fear is that it has caused them extra concern for you. It's best to say nothing else for now. All in due time, they will learn the truth."

That was enough to satisfy Helen.

"However, I will tell you this—I've enlisted Mercy's help."

"You have? With the adoption?"

"No, with Zach. It has something to do with shopping for baby clothes. I'm not going to say anything more. It'll be a surprise, and I don't want to spoil it."

"Can't you at least tell me what Mercy's going to do?"

"You'll learn all about it later. I don't want to ruin it for you."

Helen immediately started putting things together. There was an entire nursery filled with baby items that Laurel and Zach had bought for Jonathan.

The nursery. Laurel had refused to enter ever since they'd had to give up the boy they'd come to love, to think of as their own.

Helen would never forget the agonized look on her granddaughter's face as she'd handed Jonathan over to the social worker. Zach had placed his arms around Laurel, and when the door closed, they'd clung to each other and openly wept. The scene had played over and over in Helen's head for weeks afterward.

They'd carefully painted the room in preparation for the arrival of their baby boy. Zach had drawn a huge hot-air balloon with a baby in the basket. Jonathan was the name they'd chosen for him. It meant "a gift from God," and it had been scripted on the woven bucket hanging below the big, colorful balloon.

To know there was another baby due for them filled Helen with happiness. It was all she could do to keep the news to herself.

wouldn't dare attempt finding one she would use and enjoy.

At one point he'd asked for ideas, and she'd insisted she had everything she could ever want. But then her eyes had shifted to the nursery, subconsciously. Jonathan's room. Although she claimed she had everything, Zach knew better. He knew her heart's desire. A baby.

He'd badly wanted to tell her what he'd done, that he'd spoken to their caseworker at the adoption agency. If his wife knew that he'd asked that their names be reinstated she might come undone. After everything they'd been through, Laurel had given up. Zach could understand her reasons, but he didn't see why it was necessary to close the door completely. Babies did come up for adoption. When he'd first spoken to Mary, she hadn't encouraged him. But she hadn't discouraged him, either. He would keep an open mind, and he was willing to wait. Unfortunately, Laurel didn't feel the same way.

The perfect opportunity to confess what he'd done had come the night they'd gone Christmas tree shopping. That night was just like when they'd first started dating. Laurel's eyes had sparkled with laughter and Zach couldn't find it in his heart to ruin their evening with talk of the very subject that brought such pain into their lives. He couldn't do it. He recognized that Laurel suspected he was hiding something from her. He would tell her at some point, but not now. Not right before Christmas. He'd wait until after the first of the year. The timing would be better. A new year. A new hope. They could look toward the future together.

The first things to catch his eye when he entered Macy's were the festive decorations. A huge sign posted near the entrance announced B E L I E V E to all who entered the large store.

How strange that I should see that sign, Zach thought to himself. *That's what Laurel has to do. She has to believe.*

The support columns were decorated with greenery and covered with large, bright ornaments of all shapes and sizes, while other displays hung down from the ceiling, greeting the shoppers. Tall Christmas trees dominated the entrance to each department, beautifully decorated.

Zach wound his way through the throng of shoppers and found himself in the women's section. He looked at a mannequin in a beautiful red-and-white-plaid dress with gold buttons down the front and pictured his wife in it. Laurel was beautiful. He never fully understood how a woman as sweet and lovable as she was found herself attracted to a computer nerd like himself.

They'd met in college at a party where he'd felt out of place and awkward. He'd been sitting alone, nursing a beer, when she'd sat down next to him. He wanted to say something smart or funny, but his tongue seemed glued to the roof of his mouth. Laurel had taken the initiative and introduced herself, drawing him out of his shell. Their first date was in the library, studying together. Later they rode bikes around Green Lake and talked for hours. Laurel had done most of the talking, and that suited him. Zach liked the sound of her voice and marveled that she seemed to enjoy his company. He'd fallen for her immediately, and he counted his blessings every day that she'd agreed to be his wife.

With his head full of babies and the secret he was keeping from Laurel, he made his way through the store until he found himself back in front of the mannequin with the lovely dress on. It would be perfect for her. Perfect.

After he tracked down a salesclerk, he was pointed toward the appropriate rack. Zach found the size Laurel wore and swallowed hard at the price, deciding to buy it anyway. She would look stunning in it, and she deserved something new and pretty.

Pleased with his purchase, he decided to look for a special gift for Nana. He paused by the escalator to get his bearings when he realized he was next to the infant and toddler department. Pain tightened his chest.

Laurel had loved dressing Jonathan, and Nana had never been happier than when she rocked that precious baby in her arms. For a moment, he found it hard to breathe. The sense of loss felt like a kick in the gut as memories came back . . . memories of Jonathan being escorted from their home. He had wanted to shout at the unfairness of it all, but one of them needed to remain strong. On the outside, he'd put on a good front, but internally, he'd felt everything his wife had felt at that very moment, and more.

Before he could find the escalator going down, a salesclerk appeared at his side.

"Merry Christmas!" she said cheerfully, acting like he'd been the only customer that she'd had all day. "How may I help you?"

At this point the only thing Zach was thinking was how best to get out of there. This was the last department he wanted to wade through.

"Where would I find robes . . . robes like the one a grandmother would wear?" Laurel would appreciate him finding something special for Nana. She'd recently mentioned she wanted to buy her grandmother a warm robe for the winter months, with a new pair of cozy slippers, so he may as well save her the time while he was here.

The clerk sighed. "That's up on the next level, but unfortunately, the escalator broke a few minutes ago, and they've roped it off as a precaution. Something electrical, I overheard a supervisor saying. It's put quite a damper on things, with our customers all rushing around to do holiday shopping. Maintenance is on it, and hopefully it will be up and running momentarily."

"All right, then, which way to the elevator?"

"The elevator is at the opposite end of this floor, but I heard it's taking people several minutes to get on. Patience is in short supply—I'm giving you fair warning," she added sympathetically.

It appeared that this exit strategy wasn't going to work for Zach, either.

"Come with me," the saleswoman said, as though she was about to lead him to a secret passageway. She turned and fully expected Zach to follow.

Thinking the salesclerk was leading him to the stairwell, Zach obediently trailed behind her.

"As you can see, we're having a sale to end all sales. Just look at this delightful outfit." She held up a pink ruffled dress so small it could be sized only for a newborn. "Isn't this the cutest dress you've ever seen?"

Despite his discomfort, Zach smiled. The dress resembled something Scarlett O'Hara might have worn in *Gone with the Wind*. He had to admit that it was the perfect outfit to melt a daddy's heart.

"It's adorable, isn't it?" the clerk asked.

"But I . . ."

"The best part is the price tag," the clerk said, showing it to Zach.

Zach didn't have any choice but to glance at the label. It was only a few dollars. That couldn't be right. Seeing how much he'd paid for Laurel's dress, this was a mere pittance. Then again, it was for a baby, and what did he know about the cost of baby clothes?

"Who in their right mind could refuse a deal like this?" she asked.

"Yes, but as I started to say, my wife and I don't have children."

"Perhaps for a friend, then?" the woman suggested. "You're young, and I'm sure you have family or friends starting families."

Zach hesitated. Laurel had recently mentioned that one of her teacher friends was pregnant. He didn't know if the baby's sex had been determined, but he reasoned that there would likely be an opportunity down the road to give this dress away as a baby shower gift. Besides, it would be less painful for him to pick up something instead of Laurel having to.

The saleswoman appeared to be waiting for his answer.

"Yes, I suppose." Zach was beginning to feel uneasy. He wasn't sure how to extract himself from this persistent woman. He wondered if the Macy's staff was paid on commission, because she was certainly determined to make the sale.

"At this price, it's a steal, Mr. McCullough. I mean, really . . . this sale is something else. I've worked in this department for some time now, and I've never seen clothing discounted this much."

"Yes, well . . ." Zach anxiously looked around for a means of escape and found none. Then he realized that she had used his name. How on earth did she know his last name?

"Would you look at this!" The saleswoman held up a tiny western outfit. It was a blue-jean jumper with a red-checkered shirt underneath, something Annie Oakley might have worn in a sharpshooting match.

Zach smiled awkwardly. He liked this one as much as the first, though he didn't admit that out loud to the salesclerk. He feared he might be losing it. Then again, if an adoption did come through and they had a girl . . .

"How much is that one?" he found himself asking.

"It's the same price as the first dress I showed you."

"Nice," he murmured.

"I'm sure you'll want this one, too."

Too? He hadn't agreed to purchase the first dress. He had the feeling the only way to find his way out of this department was to buy the outfits and flee for his life. He looked around, surprised to find that he was the only shopper in the entire section. There'd been wall-to-wall people everywhere else in the busy store, but this department was all but deserted.

"Would you like me to wrap these items for you?"

Zach hesitated. If Laurel found out he'd spent money on baby clothes, there was no telling what she'd do. "Actually . . . uh . . . no, thank you."

The woman beamed at him, as if he was a brilliant shopper. She led the way to the checkout counter, chatting away like they were long-lost friends. Every now and again she'd pause and point out something else he was sure to need.

Zach politely refused each item, but she didn't appear to hear him. By the time they reached the register, the saleswoman had accumulated a small pile of clothes, all for a baby girl. She quickly started to ring up his purchase while he worked up his nerve to have her put everything back. Then she announced the total. He was surprised to hear that it was little more than what he'd pay for a lunch from his favorite food truck on the street below his office.

Before he completely grasped what had happened, he'd given her the cash and she handed him the beautiful red shopping bag.

"Will this be all for you this evening, Mr. McCullough? Oh, look—the escalator is working again. What great timing you seem to have."

Again, the clerk appeared to know him. Zach couldn't recall ever meeting this relentless sales-clerk, but he must have, at some point, somewhere. He was too frustrated with himself to ask, and he quickly thanked her and headed down the escalator. He slowly shook his head, lost in the events of the past few minutes. He'd been in search of a gift for Nana and ended up with a large bag of baby clothes. He couldn't have explained the last fifteen minutes if he'd wanted to.

On the sidewalk outside the store, Zach got a text from Laurel telling him the meeting with the parents was over and she was on her way home. He had no idea how he would explain to Laurel what he'd just done. He'd recklessly bought items they didn't need because they were on sale. And to think that he was the one who repeatedly told Laurel, who had a hard time resisting a good sale, that one didn't save money by spending money, no matter how good the price.

By the time he arrived home, he'd beaten himself up mentally to the point that his stomach hurt.

"I'm here," Zach announced upon crossing the threshold, without a lot of enthusiasm.

Laurel stuck her head out from inside the kitchen. "Your meeting must have gone on longer than expected."

Avoiding eye contact, Zach set the packages down on the floor as he removed his coat, hanging it up in the front closet. "The meeting let out early. I went Christmas shopping before coming home."

"It looks like you had success—why the glum face?"

"Where's Nana?" he asked, trying to divert her questions.

"She went to bed early. Mrs. Miracle left soon after I arrived home."

"Did you have dinner?" He was willing to talk about anything other than his shopping expedition. Tomorrow on his lunch break, he fully intended to return the baby clothes.

Laurel followed him into the living room. "Why aren't you looking at me?" she asked, full of concern.

Zach shrugged. He sincerely wished that his wife didn't know him so well. Unable to hide his regret, Zach's face had been a dead giveaway. Laurel knew the moment he walked in the door that he was upset.

"Zach, what's wrong?"

He wouldn't be able to brush it off. Laurel had already guessed. Trapped, he knew there was nothing to do but confess.

"I did something really stupid and I didn't want you to know."

Her concern was immediate, as well it should be. He felt like an even bigger fool for his inability to hide it from her.

She came to him and took his hand, her touch

gentle as she stared up at him, her eyes full of curiosity and concern.

Zach briefly closed his eyes, not wanting to tell her. The moment she saw the baby clothes she'd be devastated, and he wouldn't blame her.

"Did you gamble away our life savings?" she jokingly asked.

"You know me better than that."

"You lost your job?"

"No."

"Okay. You bought me an expensive Christmas gift and now you're having buyer's remorse," she said. "Zach, please tell me you didn't."

"I didn't." He recalled the dress he'd bought for his wife and determined that that was a perfectly normal secret to keep from his wife. But this was worse, much worse. He didn't know what had come over him. He wasn't an impulsive buyer. He weighed every dollar he spent. No way would he be able to explain what he'd done. He was the worst husband in the universe.

"Come on, Zach. It can't be that bad."

Getting the words out was difficult. "Like I said, my meeting got out early and I sort of got trapped in the infant and toddler department at Macy's."

The color drained from Laurel's face so fast that Zach felt the need to take hold of her shoulders and keep her upright. "I'm so sorry, baby. So sorry."

"*What* did you do?" she asked in a hoarse whisper.

"I don't know how it happened. I swear, Laurel, this salesclerk started showing me tiny outfits and for some weird reason, I couldn't help myself. She kept telling me what a huge sale it was and that the prices were beyond belief, and they were. Before I realized what had happened, I had purchased a bunch of clothes for a newborn."

Laurel covered her mouth in utter disbelief. Tears instantly sprang to her eyes.

Knowing how much his words and actions had hurt her nearly undid him. "Can you forgive me? I'll return everything first thing tomorrow."

Laurel did her best to offer him a smile, her only sign of forgiveness. Her lips trembled with the effort. "You still think . . ."

"No," he rushed to tell her. "It wasn't like that. I swear, Laurel."

"I'm not enough, am I?"

To hear her say those words nearly gutted him. "You are. I love you more than life itself, Laurel, I swear it."

Her throat worked with a hard swallow as she nodded. "You'll return everything?"

"I promise. Everything goes back first thing tomorrow."

She wiped a stray tear from her cheek and accepted his apology. "I guess we're more alike than I realized."

"How so?"

"You couldn't resist a good sale, after all."

CHAPTER NINE

Helen knew something was wrong. She heard Laurel and Zach talking, and even from this distance she could tell they were arguing. Because her hearing wasn't as good as it had once been, Helen was unable to make out the gist of what had happened.

What bothered Helen the most, however, was knowing there was a problem. Her instinct was to climb out of bed and find out what was wrong. The temptation was strong. Instead, she'd sat on the edge of her bed and weighed her options. The only drawback to having Laurel and Zach live with her had been knowing when to step in and offer help, and when to leave matters be. She concluded that the young couple didn't need or want her to interfere.

The following morning, Helen woke thirty minutes before Laurel was scheduled to leave for school. Her granddaughter sat at the table, mindlessly stirring oatmeal in her bowl, when Helen came into the kitchen.

"Good morning," she said, closely watching this grown woman whom she'd raised from the age of ten.

"Morning, Nana," Laurel said, hurriedly getting up from her chair. "Sit down and let me get you some tea."

Helen took a seat at the table. She would need to be blind to not notice Laurel's pale face and the absentminded way she moved about the kitchen.

"Are you feeling all right?" Helen asked, carefully approaching the subject. "This is flu season and you being with the children all day at school . . ."

"I'm fine."

Her response offered no reassurance.

"You've barely touched your oatmeal," Helen said.

"I don't have much of an appetite."

Laurel set the tea in front of Helen and sat down.

Unsure how hard to press her granddaughter, Helen waited a few minutes while she carefully sipped the hot liquid. She mulled over if her prying would do more harm than good until she could bear it no longer and had to know.

"Is everything all right between you and Zach?"

"Nana," Laurel immediately protested. "What makes you ask that? We're fine. Zach is the best thing that ever happened to me . . . I . . ." Her voice faded away.

"I know, I know . . . I thought I heard you two disagreeing about something. I must've been mistaken."

Looking away, Laurel didn't deny or confirm. "It was a silly thing. Something he regrets. Zach is making it right today." Laurel hesitated, as if she should say more, then blurted out, "I need to get to school," scooting back her chair. "Mrs. Miracle will be here any moment." Laurel took her bowl to the sink, dumped the contents in the garbage disposal, and set the bowl in the dishwasher. Kissing Helen on the cheek, she headed into the other room and was soon gone.

Sad, and wishing she could've been of more help, Helen continued to sit and drink her tea. She wondered what it was that Zach had done. He was a thoughtful person, and Helen knew he would never do anything to intentionally hurt Laurel.

It wasn't long before the front door opened and her Caring Angel arrived.

"Good morning! It's a new day!" Mrs. Miracle cheerfully swept into the kitchen, wearing a bright smile. She always arrived with an agenda in hand. After giving Helen an hour or two each morning for knitting and chatting, they'd often plan an outing. They'd been to play bingo at the senior center one day. Then another time, they'd bundled up to watch the ferries come in and out of the port from Alki Point while having a bite to eat at a small Hawaiian-Korean fusion café. And then there was the afternoon they ventured out to a holiday craft sale at a local church. Helen hadn't been this active in what felt like years. If she was right, today was the planned trip to Hobby Lobby for more yarn. The baby booties were finished, and she needed more yarn for a matching blanket. Helen enjoyed these outings with her companion, loving that she had this caring woman beside her the entire time. She never tired of seeing the loving glow on her face. It reminded her daily that Mrs. Miracle had arrived from heaven.

"Did you have a good night's sleep, Helen?"

"Unfortunately not." She couldn't rest knowing her granddaughter was miserable.

Whirling around, Mrs. Miracle looked perplexed. "Why ever not?"

No need to hide anything from Mrs. Miracle.

"I was worried about Laurel and Zach. Did you happen to pass Laurel on your way in?"

"I didn't. Is there a problem?" She looked genuinely concerned.

Caught up in her thoughts, Helen barely heard the question. After a moment, she responded. "I don't know what it could be. Sometimes I can hear Laurel and Zach talking, and I can't help but listen. Last night, they seemed to be purposefully keeping their voices down so I couldn't make out what they were saying."

"I see."

"I didn't mean to be prying, but I couldn't stand to see her upset, so I asked. Laurel said Zach had done something foolish but would be making it right today. She didn't go into details. It looked for a minute like she wanted to explain but didn't. Whatever it was devastated her. I can't imagine Zach doing anything to purposely upset her like this."

Mrs. Miracle reached across the table and gently squeezed Helen's hand. "I believe I know the problem."

Helen immediately looked up from her teacup.

"I suspect this has something to do with Zach's downtown shopping spree at Macy's last evening after his meeting."

Zach had gone Christmas shopping? This was news to Helen. Even though it was relatively early, Helen had been tired from their outing earlier that day and had headed to bed before he had arrived home. She'd drifted off to sleep almost immediately and awoke when she'd heard their voices, hushed and heated.

"But Laurel is the one who enjoys shopping," Helen said, unable to understand what had led Zach to enter a busy downtown department store in the height of the holiday season.

"Well," Mrs. Miracle started, looking pleased with herself, "I can't say what exactly it was that upset Laurel, but I believe Zach met up with a friend of mine last evening."

"A friend? Of yours?"

Mrs. Miracle's eyes sparked with mischief. "A very good friend."

"Might I ask . . ." Helen ventured. "Might this have been one of the heavenly friends you mentioned earlier?"

The other woman's responding smile said it all.

Helen's eyes widened even as she lowered her voice. "Zach met an angel? In Macy's? But if that's the case, then why did this upset Laurel and why is Zach determined to make it right?"

"Oftentimes when God works, what happens makes no sense. It will all come together down the road. Trust me on this."

None of this made sense to Helen, but she was willing to do as her friend asked. In time it would be revealed, and she would understand. For now, that had to be enough.

CHAPTER TEN

"I don't understand," Zach said, staring at the young salesclerk. "I purchased these baby outfits myself, less than twenty-four hours ago. I have the sales slip right here, and I would like to return them." He could hear mumbled complaints coming from the line of customers behind him, which he did his best to ignore.

The woman gave him a look reserved for someone trying to take advantage of the store's return policy. "But that isn't possible."

"It *is* possible," Zach said through gritted teeth. Normally, he was an easygoing kind of guy, but this clerk was testing every ounce of patience he had. He couldn't understand why he was having problems returning the baby clothes that he'd purchased the day before.

"Those items you claim to have purchased yesterday with cash haven't been carried by Macy's for months now. To insist that you bought them yesterday isn't possible."

"But . . ." Apparently, he didn't have a leg to stand on, according to the salesclerk. In his eagerness to get out of the store the day before, he hadn't bothered to look at the receipt. The faded ink on the receipt kept him from proving the date of his purchase.

The clerk glanced past him to the line of customers.

Zach turned away and received several irritated looks. Nothing that the clerk said added up. He put the receipt back into the bag and reluctantly walked away. He'd used his lunch break to try to make the return, so he made the quick three-minute walk back to his office.

Sitting in front of his computer, he opened the bag and removed the top garment. Despite his irritation at his lack of success, he smiled. He had to admit, this was by far the coolest little cowgirl outfit.

He glanced at the label attached to it and did an Internet search. Sure enough, he discovered the company had been bought out by a larger company nine months earlier and the brand name no longer existed. He also checked Macy's website, and none of the company's items were available. All the other things he'd purchased were from the same company—no longer in existence, no longer being sold at Macy's.

The cowgirl outfit remained on the top of his desk. Unbidden, the image of a baby girl filled his thoughts, happy and cooing as Laurel gently rocked her. He tried to cast it away, but the vision was clear and concise, and the images wouldn't go away.

A sense of loss and emptiness settled over him, weighing him down like concrete boots. Perhaps because he wanted a family as keenly as Laurel once had, he hadn't been able to return the baby items for a reason. A very good reason. Maybe he was meant to have them.

His heart started to race. Could it be that this was a sign? Was this a God-given sign that they were about to receive an infant? He wanted to believe. Desperately so. Thinking back on all the failed attempts for a family didn't inspire his faith. He hated to be weak, but he needed something to help him believe. A sign that would tell him he hadn't completely lost touch with reality.

Zach had never been much of a praying man. He attended church and recited the liturgy, but as for personal prayers, he felt awkward and self-conscious. But he was willing to give it a try. He bowed his head in the confines of his cubicle and silently prayed. "God. Hi . . . It's me."

He felt foolish addressing God so casually. God was *God*, not a beer buddy. With determination, he started again. "Dear Lord, I don't have a lot of fancy words, so I'm going to speak plainly. You know my heart. You know how much I love Laurel, so I'm asking that if a baby really is coming, then please give me a sign. You don't need to move mountains or black out the sky, or anything like that. A small sign will do. I need something to get me over this hump of disbelief, something simple that will help me to believe. Laurel doesn't need to know. If You think it's best, I won't say a word to her until the time is right. Thank you. Thank you for Laurel and for Nana and for Mrs. Miracle and for all You've done for me already. Forgive my lack of faith. Amen."

Right at the end of his prayer, a coworker, Joel, strolled past his desk. "Don't forget the white-elephant gift exchange this afternoon."

"I'll be there," Zach replied, jerking guiltily.

"You okay, buddy?"

"Sure. Sure. I'll be there."

The polka-dot sweater from the year before was wrapped and ready. This was a fun game their group did each Christmas. Like the rest of the department, he went along with it.

Settling back to work, Zach let his thoughts wander to Laurel and the baby clothes. The best thing he could think to do was hide them until the time was right. In retrospect, he was glad he'd paid for them with cash. That was a blessing in disguise, as she couldn't look for a return on their credit card statement.

He looked down at the carefully crafted red bag at his feet, when the phone rang at his desk, bringing him back to reality. "Zach McCullough."

"Hello, Zach. This is Mary Swindoll."

Zach straightened in his chair. It was the case-worker from the adoption agency. This was it. The sign he'd asked for. God had heard his prayer and he was about to receive the news of an available baby for their family.

His pulse raced so hard and fast that the sound echoed in his ears. "Yes?"

"I hope it's fine that I called you at work. You mentioned that Laurel isn't able to receive phone calls at school, so I thought it best to reach out to you."

"Do you have a baby for us?" he blurted out.

A short, uncomfortable silence followed. "No, Zach. I'm sorry. I'm calling for another reason."

His spirits dove, landing in a dark pit. He clenched his jaw and closed his eyes. If he didn't battle these feelings, he'd become a victim of despair.

"How may I help you?" he asked, his voice devoid of emotion.

Mary spoke for several minutes about how they were planning to update the agency's website, and that they wanted to share the stories of couples at each stage of the adoption process: new applicants, couples in the waiting process, couples who'd had initial disappointments, and couples who'd had success. She wanted to see if Zach and Laurel would be willing to be interviewed and photographed for the website.

"We think it will give a realistic picture of the adoption process, with real faces and real stories. You and Laurel have had your share of ups and downs, and I think you two would be the perfect couple to talk about your experiences. Would you be willing to participate? It'd be a great help to other couples starting out. We'll understand your decision, one way or the other."

"Ah . . ." Zach's head was spinning. Their caseworker didn't know he hadn't told Laurel about renewing their application. "I . . . I don't think that would work for us." He floundered over the words.

"It would mean a great deal to other couples with your experience."

"I know, but—"

"I understand," Mary inserted. "Talk it over with Laurel."

"Okay, but I still don't think this is something we'll want to do."

"I understand," she repeated, undiscouraged. "I do. But you're the perfect couple for this. All I'm asking is that you and Laurel discuss this and get back to me."

"All right," he said, his words heavy with reluctance.

"I'll look forward to hearing from you. Thank you, Zach."

"Before you go," he said, stopping her. "May I ask you something?"

"Of course."

"I don't know if you can answer this. I feel a bit foolish pressing the point, but it would mean a great deal to us if you could give us an idea of how much longer an adoption may take. Do you realistically think there's even a remote chance of an infant becoming available anytime soon?"

Silence followed as he waited for Mary to answer. He could sense her hesitation.

"I do know of a high school girl who's made the decision to have an open adoption. She came into the agency a few days ago with her parents. I haven't spoken with the caseworker who's worked with the family. I've heard it's been a difficult decision for them, and from what I understand, she's due any day now. A Christmas baby. There's no greater gift, is there?"

"There isn't," Zach agreed. He couldn't keep the optimism swelling up inside of him under control. Unseen, and unknown, he desired this child. He thought about that bag of clothes sitting under his desk.

"Would you happen to know if it's a boy or a girl?"

"From what I understand, it is a girl."

"Is there any possibility—" His question came to a halt, and he left the rest unsaid. Mary knew what he was asking.

"I'm sorry, Zach," she said, her voice full of regret. "From what I heard, the birth mother has already chosen a family."

Just as quickly as hope had risen in his heart, it died.

"I know how difficult and drawn-out this process can sometimes be," Mary said sympathetically. "All I can suggest is to be patient."

He inhaled, determined to remain strong. Yes, he had to hang on. "Thanks, Mary," he said, and after exchanging genuine Christmas greetings, he ended the call.

Sitting at his desk, Zach fought discouragement.

As Mary said, all they needed was patience. Only patience was in short supply.

With a determined effort, Zach returned to the work in front of him, and the afternoon flew past. He didn't even notice that his coworkers had left for the white-elephant exchange.

"Hey, Zach—it's time," Joel said, slapping the back of his chair.

Zach looked away from his computer screen and glanced up. "Time?"

"The Christmas party."

"Oh yeah." He closed his computer for the day, pulled out the gift-wrapped box he'd brought from home, and joined his coworkers in the conference room.

The staff milled around, sampling the desserts and finger foods that had been delivered from the catering company. With Christmas upon them, there was general chatter about holiday plans.

The party was festive, and his coworkers joked while sampling the appetizers and sweets. Zach skipped the chocolates and decorated sugar cookies, choosing instead the small triangular sandwiches. Because he'd made the run to the department store, he'd skipped lunch and was hungry for food with substance.

When it came time for the white-elephant exchange, they each drew numbers. Out of the twenty-five staff members present, Zach drew number sixteen. Some of the gifts were expertly wrapped; others were in holiday bags, and the gifts brought in by most of the single guys were wrapped in brown grocery bags. All were piled in the center of the conference table.

He knew better than to go for the pretty boxes. They had always proven to be notoriously bad choices, which was a lesson he'd learned when he'd gotten stuck with a pink polka-dot sweater. When his turn came, he took a plain gift, small and rectangular.

When he opened it, he stopped and looked up, surprised to find it was a cigar box.

"What's inside?" someone yelled out.

Not knowing what to expect, he opened it and gasped. Inside was row upon row of cigars with preprinted pink labels. Each one exclaimed, in large letters, IT'S A GIRL. His hand froze and his throat thickened, and he found he was unable to speak. This was it. The answer to his prayer. He'd asked God for a sign and He had given him one.

"The wife had a son," Joel Perkins explained out loud, attempting to cover the awkward silence. "We chose not to know the sex of the baby beforehand, so to be prepared, I ordered cigar boxes for both a boy and a girl."

Zach managed a grin and set the cigars on the tabletop. He resisted the temptation to look upward and silently thank God. Once his pulse returned to normal, he felt like he could walk on air.

As he headed home, Zach continued to reason with himself and rationalize his actions. He'd already decided not to tell Laurel he hadn't returned the baby clothes. Nor was he comfortable sharing with her what he'd received in the white-elephant exchange. Both would hurt her. Rather than rub salt in her wounds, he decided to hide the cigars along with the baby clothes. That would be best all the way around, he reasoned to himself. If she did ask, he'd find a way to sidestep her questions.

He recalled with relief that she was staying after school today for parent-teacher meetings. If he could tuck them away in the nursery before she got home, Laurel would never find either the clothes or the cigars. She never went into that room. Not since Jonathan left.

As luck would have it, the commute home was worse than normal. Even the bus driver was becoming impatient with the unusually heavy traffic. As the bus came to a halt at every red light, Zach impatiently bounced his knee in irritation, waiting for the signal to change. Normally the ride home relaxed him. He would read or close his eyes and go with the flow. Not so this evening. He was on a mission to arrive before Laurel.

From the bus stop, he nearly raced the two blocks to the house. The garage door was shut, and he couldn't even see if her car was there. Bounding up the porch steps and through the front door, he found Helen knitting in her favorite chair and Mrs. Miracle sitting next to her. Helen had a bundle of pink yarn at her side and was intently working her knitting needles.

"Is Laurel home?" he asked breathlessly.

"Not yet," Helen said, looking at him quizzically. "My goodness, Zach, where's the fire?"

"I'll explain in a minute." He dashed into the

nursery and tucked the clothes and cigars into the bottom drawer of the dresser. Confident that his secret was secure, he quickly closed the drawer and exited.

With both items safely out of sight, he gave a huge sigh of relief and joined the ladies in the living room. He prayed he had pulled this off without Laurel ever knowing.

Mrs. Miracle, he noticed, paid avid attention to her knitting, wearing a rather amused smile, while Nana studied Zach, her eyes wide with curiosity.

"What was *that* all about?" Helen asked, setting her knitting aside.

"Long story," Zach replied, unwilling to explain.

Helen's face softened. "You got a special Christmas gift for Laurel, and you wanted to hide it before she got home. You're so thoughtful, Zach. I'm glad she has you in her life."

Zach pretended to ignore Helen's compliment, which, with his guilt, didn't feel like one.

"How did the white-elephant exchange go this afternoon?" Mrs. Miracle asked.

Zach snapped his head around toward the older woman. He didn't recall mentioning anything about the gift exchange to her or to Helen.

Mrs. Miracle continued to nonchalantly tug away on her skein of yarn, awaiting his reply.

"It went fine," he said, being as vague as possible.

"Oh yes, the gift exchange," Helen said. "Laurel mentioned you were taking that funny-looking polka-dot sweater you got last Christmas."

"I did."

"What crazy gift did you get this time around?"

The direct question was difficult to avoid, so he mustered up a generic reply. "It was something goofy, as usual."

"But a useful one," Mrs. Miracle added, seeming to have some sort of insider information. "Something you might well need, and soon."

"Perhaps," Zach said with a confused look on his face. She made it sound like she knew what he'd unwrapped at the office gift exchange that afternoon.

Mrs. Miracle laid aside her knitting. A serious look came over her face. "Zach, you do realize that God hears our prayers, don't you?"

He stared at her, surprised by her question. Was she implying that she knew all about his prayer at his desk that afternoon? Maybe he and Laurel had taken this stranger at face value, never questioning her sudden appearance at their front door. Granted, Mrs. Miracle was doing a great job with Laurel's grandmother, but that wasn't the problem. This woman seemed to know far more than she should. Something wasn't right. Zach silently determined that it was time to check into her background and find out who exactly this woman was.

CHAPTER ELEVEN

When Laurel awoke, Zach was already down in the kitchen getting their morning coffee ready, earlier than normal. Slipping out of bed, she quickly showered and dressed, then headed down to the kitchen.

"I'm surprised you're ready this early," Zach said as he fixed the collar on his shirt and threw a pull-on sweater over his head while she poured a cup of coffee.

"I need to get to the school early," she reminded him. With the holiday program just days away there were several loose ends she needed to take care of, and mornings were her best time. By the end of the school day, she was rattle-brained, and she worried that she might overlook something. She wanted to kick herself for volunteering to oversee the entire program. What had she been thinking?

"How's the production shaping up?"

Laurel took that first restorative sip. "About as good as can be expected."

"I meant to tell you the other day—I got the time off, so I'll be there."

"You did?" For him to ask for time off at this time of year was big, and she hadn't asked him to go, not wanting to put any extra pressure on him. Although he rarely spoke about his own commitments when it came to work, she knew he was heading up a large project with pending deadlines.

"I'm so glad."

His bagel popped up from the toaster, and he offered Laurel a shy smile. He added cream cheese and took his first bite.

"I hate to put anything more on your plate, Laurel, but I need you to do something for me." His forehead creased with a thick frown. "I wouldn't ask if I didn't feel strongly about it."

"What do you need?"

Zach set his bagel aside and looked down at it like the poppy seeds on top were ready to offer him insight and wisdom. "That first agency you called, asking about hiring a home companion for your grandmother . . ."

"Yes, the Caring Angels. What about it?"

"Would you contact them again and ask about Mrs. Miracle's references? Something doesn't feel right about her."

"You don't like Mrs. Miracle?"

"Helen told me her real name is Merkel. Be sure and give that name to the agency."

"I will. But why? What aren't you telling me?" As

far as Laurel was concerned, the woman had been nothing but wonderful. "Did something happen last night that I don't know about?" Maybe this was why Zach had been acting so strange.

"Well, for one thing, she claims she's an angel."

"But did *she* make that claim?" Laurel returned, confused by his need to dig into their home companion's work history. "It's *Nana* who insisted on that. Not Mrs. Miracle or Merkel—whatever name she goes by." Laurel didn't mean to sound defensive, but the woman had been an answer to their prayers. The changes in Nana since Mrs. Miracle's arrival were night and day. Hiring the companion had made all the difference in the world. Laurel could leave for school each day with all the worry lifted from her shoulders.

"Please, just call. I swear there's something fishy about her. I think we need to find out what we can, just to make sure your grandmother is in good hands when we leave. We never checked her story or asked about her previous work history, not to mention all this hullabaloo about her being an angel."

"But you were the one who told me that if Nana wanted to believe her caregiver was an angel, then we should let her."

"Of course, I remember."

"I still don't understand why all this concern. What aren't you telling me?"

He didn't answer, and Laurel could tell he was struggling to put his thoughts into words.

"Zach," she said, doing her best to remain calm

and reasonable. "You have to agree that Mrs. Miracle has been exactly what Nana needed."

Zach's shoulders lifted with a sigh and he turned away from her. Something strange was going on. Laurel couldn't put her finger on it. He was hiding something from her; she was certain of it. Her suspicions had been aroused in the last few weeks, but she'd convinced herself it was her imagination. There'd been nothing overt, just this distance she'd been feeling. An emotional distance. He'd been on edge—jumpy—like he was keeping a secret. She trusted him completely, or so she thought. A brief thought of an affair had crossed her mind, but she refused to believe it. She almost laughed at the thought of it, knowing that neither of them could afford an affair, let alone desire another person. Still, she felt something was off with her husband. Way off. She knew she needed to get to the bottom of whatever it was. She'd confront him this evening.

He turned to face her. "I understood you like Mrs. Miracle. I do, too. If you must know, she seems to know things that she shouldn't."

"Such as?"

"Please, Laurel, just call them. If you can't, I'll make a point to do it myself, but you were the one who filled out the application and talked to the agency in the first place. I'd rather you did this."

"All right, I'll make the call."

"Thank you." With a quick kiss on her cheek, Zach headed out the door.

Laurel reached for the half-bagel he'd left behind. As she chewed, she reconsidered Zach's request. What he said was true. Laurel had felt it herself. The caregiver did seem to know far more about their circumstances than what Nana might have shared with her.

The home companion wasn't anything like what Laurel had expected. All the extra hours Mrs. Miracle had put in were remarkable, especially when she insisted that she wouldn't need to be paid overtime. Then there were the homemade meals every night when they came home from work. The extra effort to make Nana's daily life more enjoyable, with the addition of outings that Nana truly seemed to enjoy.

Now that she thought about it, Laurel saw other oddities. The unexpectedness of her arrival that first evening, without an advance call from the agency. The Christmas tree, extravagantly decorated. And the lost ornaments from years gone by, especially the crumbled, precious homemade bell that had miraculously reappeared out of nowhere. It couldn't possibly be the same ornament. And yet there it was, hanging on the tree again.

Details started adding up in her head. Questions that defied answers. Unusual events that seemed impossible.

Zach was right. There was good reason for Laurel to contact the agency and find out what she could about her grandmother's caregiver.

CHAPTER TWELVE

Helen lingered in bed that morning. It was warm and cozy under the blankets, and she didn't feel much incentive to get up and get dressed for some reason.

"Helen?" Mrs. Miracle called from the living room. "It's almost ten."

Helen glanced at the clock, surprised to see how quickly the morning had evaporated. She realized she had been drifting in and out of sleep.

"How did you sleep, dear?" her companion asked upon entering Helen's room. Mrs. Miracle sat on the edge of Helen's bed with a concerned look on her face.

"Lazy," Helen admitted, stretching her arms above her head and yawning.

"Then rest. I've led you on a merry chase the last few days. We might have overdone our walk to the senior center yesterday."

"The fresh air did me good," Helen replied, "and I enjoyed reconnecting with old friends." It'd been wonderful to see so many of her friends. Helen hadn't realized how isolated she'd become. She'd been afraid to venture out on her own even though the senior center was within easy walking distance.

In the short time she'd been with Helen, Mrs. Miracle had expanded her world. The senior center was full of activities and events. Before Mrs. Miracle had arrived, Helen had hibernated in the house alone, growing wary and depressed without realizing what was happening or why. No wonder her brain cells were dying off. They hadn't been fed anything more than daytime television. Just yesterday, while playing bingo, she'd run into her dear friend, Mary Lou, who'd once lived in the neighborhood. It'd been delightful to reconnect.

"Oh goodness," Helen exclaimed when she suddenly realized what day it was. "Is this Laurel's big day at the school? I need to get up and get ready." Helen knew how important this holiday program Laurel was overseeing was to her granddaughter.

"That's not until tomorrow, love."

"Oh, good. No way am I missing it. Laurel would never forgive me, and I wouldn't forgive myself!" Helen tossed aside the covers and climbed out of the bed with some help from Mrs. Miracle. Laurel had talked of little else but this massive production involving the entire elementary school. Each class contributed in some way, with either a skit or a singing performance. The school band, as young as the children were, would be playing as well. Her granddaughter had worked hard, spending countless hours of her own time to ensure that the performance would be entertaining not only for the students but for the myriad family and friends who would be attending.

Helen finished dressing. She felt energized and excited for Laurel, and for Christmas. She'd done more this year to prepare for Christmas than she had in recent memory—baking cookies, preparing the Christmas cards, decorating the tree, socializing with old friends and new—and it was all due to her angel friend. The Christmas tree, however, stood out above all else.

Funny thing, that tree. Helen had wanted to work right alongside Mrs. Miracle with the decorating. She'd tired quickly, however, and decided to rest in her chair. She'd only briefly closed her eyes—or so she thought. When she looked up again, the entire tree was finished and marvelously decorated.

In mere minutes. It would be impossible for that to have happened in such a short time, yet Helen had witnessed it herself. She decided that it had to be a trick—some sort of angel trick. She would have doubted such a thing were possible if it hadn't happened right in front of her.

Once in the kitchen, Helen took a seat at the kitchen table. Ever helpful, Mrs. Miracle placed a cup of tea in front of Helen, along with a single slice of toast, smothered with her favorite raspberry jam.

"You'd better eat something if we're going to be gallivanting off to new adventures."

"That is a *perfect* description of what we've been

doing ever since you arrived, isn't it? Gallivanting," Helen said, smiling over the top of her teacup. The warm liquid soothed her throat. Oh, how she enjoyed her morning tea. Orange pekoe. She must mention it to Mary Lou, who she knew loved tea as much as she did.

Mrs. Miracle sat across from Helen. "How are you feeling today?"

"Wonderful. I've made plans with Mary Lou to stop by after the holidays, and we've made a date to play Scrabble. She's a knitter, and from what she says, she has quite the stash of yarn." But then, in her opinion, one could never have too much yarn.

Mrs. Miracle wore a silly grin, holding back some amusement, then covered her mouth and giggled before shaking her head at Helen.

Helen stared at her quizzically and raised one delicate brow.

Setting the teacup aside, her companion saw the look. "You need to forgive me. I was thinking about something rather entertaining. Laurel will be calling the agency today to check on my references and employment history."

"She's doing *what*?" It was far from humorous to Helen. She was upset that her friend's credentials would be in question. "Whatever for?"

"Zach and Laurel have concerns about me."

Helen noticed that Mrs. Miracle showed no signs of distress. "Concerns about what?" She wished Laurel had asked for her opinion. Helen had no complaints at all. In fact, she was eternally grateful for Mrs. Miracle, and now considered her a close friend. It distressed her that those two had gone behind her back about this.

As though reading her thoughts, Mrs. Miracle held up her hand. "No worries, love. I'm afraid I might have brought this on myself."

"You? What could you have possibly done to warrant this?"

Leaning back in her chair, the other woman sobered. "I mentioned something to Zach that I should have kept to myself. That young man is a quick study. Don't worry, Helen, there's no need for concern. It's being handled. All is well."

That left Helen with even more questions. "Did you slip and tell him about the baby?"

"No, not directly. It was something I implied. Some mention of the future, but Zach picked up on it right away. I'm afraid there are times when my tongue gets ahead of my brain."

"But . . ."

"Yes, yes, I know. I'm an angel, but when I hang with humans for long, I seem to pick up a few of your less favorable human traits. Saying more than I should is one of them."

"Really? What did you let slip?"

"Well, for one," she said thoughtfully, tapping her index finger against her lower lip, "I should never have told you about Shirley, Goodness, and Mercy. At times, and this is embarrassing to admit, I forget I'm an angel. I know that sounds ridiculous, but I fear it's true. And at other times, I overstep my boundaries. That's what happened with Zach."

"Overstep? How so?"

"I knew you were going to ask me that," Mrs. Miracle said, looking chagrined. She smoothed out the napkin on her lap, avoiding eye contact. "It's all due to what happened earlier in the week. I'm afraid I laid it on rather thick."

Clearly more had been going on than Helen knew.

"I arranged for Zach to buy baby clothes, with Mercy's help. Then I heard from Mercy that he'd prayed for a sign from God that he was doing the right thing, so the two of us conspired to answer his prayer. That's how he ended up with a box of cigars individually wrapped with pink IT'S A GIRL labels at the gift exchange. It *was* a bit over the top, now that I look back on it." She paused and giggled. "I just couldn't help myself, and Mercy was all in. I thought it was the perfect answer to his doubts."

"If it makes you feel any better, I think the box of cigars was a nice touch," Helen said.

"Perhaps, but later when he came home, I implied to him what he'd received that afternoon in the exchange was something he'd be able to put to good use in the future. The way Zach saw it, I shouldn't have had any way of knowing what that gift was. See now? I was getting ahead of myself, yet again. That aroused his suspicions, which is why he asked Laurel to contact the agency."

While her friend didn't appear overly distressed, Helen worried about the possible consequences of such a call. After all, Helen was no longer convinced that Mrs. Miracle had arrived by conventional hiring practices.

"Will Laurel discover something you'd rather she not?" Helen asked, rubbing her hands together in nervous agitation.

"Well . . . possibly. The agency that sent me isn't exactly the one your granddaughter first contacted."

"I didn't think it would be. Is there any way to divert the call to the . . . the 'proper' channels?"

"Where there's a will, there's a way, especially if you're an angel. My friend Shirley—Shirley of the 'Shirley, Goodness, and Mercy' stories I've mentioned—took care of the matter. She's stepping in as a receptionist and will answer Laurel's questions. I am confident Laurel will be reassured, although I'm upset with myself."

"Whatever for?"

"Sometimes I simply can't help myself," Mrs. Miracle added. "Zach needed confirmation and he got it, thanks in large part to Mercy. I should have left matters alone. That's another unfortunate human trait I've acquired while on earth: impatience."

"Will I have the opportunity to meet your angel friends someday? You've told me so much about them."

"All in good time, my dear. All in good time."

"And I'll have the chance to hold my great-granddaughter in my arms, won't I?"

"Oh yes, and she's going to love you, as much as Laurel does."

To know that she would have the opportunity to see the joy on Laurel's face as she held her daughter in her arms—a baby who wouldn't be taken away—was far more than Helen had prayed for.

The two moved into the living room and began to work on their knitting projects, chatting about the future as Helen's fingers worked the pink yarn into what would be a blanket for her great-granddaughter. She knit with a sense of purpose, wanting it to be ready for the baby.

Laurel waited until lunchtime before she placed a call to Caring Angels. She closed the door to her classroom so she wouldn't be interrupted, and took out the business card Mrs. Miracle had given her with the agency phone number on it

"Caring Angels," the receptionist answered in a professional yet cheerful tone. "This is Shirley. How may I help you?"

"Shirley," Laurel repeated, wondering how best to start this awkward conversation. "This is Laurel McCullough. I don't recall speaking with you when I originally contacted the agency. I believe it was a Ms. Jones. Elise, if I'm not mistaken. Is she available to answer a few questions?"

In the same helpful tone, the receptionist didn't hesitate. "Ms. Jones isn't available right now, but I'm familiar with your name, Mrs. McCullough."

"Oh . . . I'd hoped to speak with Ms. Jones." Feeling uncomfortable, Laurel nibbled on her lower lip.

"Although I'm fairly new to Caring Angels, I'm sure I'll be able to answer any questions you might have," the receptionist responded with confidence. "I have all the information at my fingertips."

Laurel started to explain the reason for her call, but the overly competent receptionist interrupted.

"I do believe it was Mrs. Merkel we placed with your grandmother. Helen Fischer is your grandmother's name, correct? Yes, I see that indeed, it was Mrs. Merkel that we placed with Helen. Mrs. Merkel became available and we dispatched her right away. Is there a problem?"

"No . . . not a problem. That's not the word I'd use."

"A concern, perhaps?"

"Something like that." Laurel wasn't exactly sure where to start. "My nana believes Mrs. Miracle—she asked us to call her Mrs. Miracle, not Merkel—my grandmother believes that her home companion is . . . is . . . well, she believes that Mrs. Miracle is an angel." Might as well mention that as an opener and get it out of the way.

Shirley made a soft sighing sound. "We hear that often, Mrs. McCullough. Many of our elderly patients feel that those employed by our agency are earthly angels, as we do our utmost to provide the best care in the industry."

"I'm not talking about a human angel, as in someone who is kind and caring," Laurel rushed to explain. "My grandmother believes Mrs. Merkel is a *real* angel. A heavenly angel sent by God. You know . . . an *angel* angel."

A short silence followed. "I see. Yes, well . . . there are times when the two can easily be confused, especially with one who is experiencing a decline in memory and reality."

Laurel decided she was handling this all wrong and determined that she'd need to switch her approach to a more direct one. "Would you be able to share any background information you have on Mrs. Merkel? I'm embarrassed to admit we were so relieved when she showed up at our door that evening that, quite frankly, we overlooked checking her references." Knowing the agency had such an excellent reputation in the area, Laurel and Zach had justified their oversight.

"Certainly. Let me pull up the HR files on her."

Laurel heard the click of the computer keys. Shirley seemed to be reading to herself, as several seconds of silence followed.

"All right, I have it here in front of me. Ask me what you'd like to know."

"How long has Mrs. Merkel been with the agency?" Laurel asked, seeing that this was probably a good place to start.

"Well, that should be easy enough to answer." This was followed by another short pause. "It appears," Shirley said, sighing, "that Mrs. Merkel is relatively new to us, although I see here that she came with glowing reports and recommendations from previous clients at other agencies where she's worked."

This didn't surprise Laurel.

"What were her previous positions before she came to work for Caring Angels?"

"Let me check. I'll need to scroll down to her work history, so give me a minute," Shirley said, sounding efficient and helpful. "I'm not as familiar as I should be with this computer yet. They are terribly out-of-date compared to what we're accustomed to in"—she stumbled over her words—"well, compared to where I was last employed."

Laurel thought it peculiar that the agency would use antiquated equipment, but she kept the comment to herself.

"All right. Here it is. Prior to her assignment at your home, Mrs. Merkel was employed as a nanny. For a single father. He gave her a glowing recommendation."

There was that word again: *glowing.*

"So, she was a nanny," Laurel repeated. That made sense, because Mrs. Miracle was a nurturing woman.

"I see here that she's been working as a caregiver for some time now. Her files show that she's had plenty of experience working with the elderly. If there's a problem, please let us know, as it's important that we provide care that's above and beyond our customers' expectations."

"That's just it," Laurel said. The woman had found the words she hadn't been able to say.

"What do you mean?"

"She has met our expectations far beyond what we planned. But . . ." Laurel struggled to find the right words. "It's a bit hard to explain. She seems to *know* things . . . things she shouldn't know. Things about my grandmother, about my husband and me . . . It's all rather, well, *uncanny* is the word I'd use."

" 'Know things'?" Shirley repeated thoughtfully.

"Do you think any of this information might actually be coming from your grandmother? You know how it is with the elderly . . . They've often lost that filter when it comes to sharing family issues."

That was something to consider, although it wouldn't explain what had happened with the Christmas tree and the unusual reappearance of the Christmas decorations that had once been considered long lost or long gone.

"I don't think—"

She was cut off when Shirley interrupted her. "Oh my. Well, *this* is interesting." The receptionist had apparently continued to read Mrs. Miracle's file.

"What?" Laurel sat up straight, pressing the phone to her ear, convinced she was about to learn something important.

"This particular recommendation. It comes directly from a well-known celebrity." Her voice dipped. "He's an actor and he couldn't seem to say enough good things about her. How often does a person of that stature take the time to write a letter of recommendation? Now, *that* must tell you something," Shirley continued. "And the amazing things he wrote about her! Oh my. You'd think she'd done something extraordinarily special to have warranted this letter."

"Another *glowing* report, I'm assuming?"

The receptionist laughed. "Yes, I'd say so. Are there any other questions you have, Mrs. McCullough?"

"Is there anything in the files where former clients have mentioned any unusual behaviors or unique abilities she may have?"

Click went the computer keys. "Everything listed here states that she's exactly the type of person we hope to employ. Mrs. Miracle goes above and beyond a client's expectations when it comes to those in her care. Does that reassure you, or is there something else?"

"No . . . not really. I suppose that answers all my questions," Laurel said, only slightly reassured. She didn't know how it was possible that this caregiver could be so perfect in every way.

"There's absolutely nothing in her employment files that should give you any cause to worry. It appears your grandmother is in excellent hands."

"You're right," Laurel said. "Thank you for your time, Shirley. I apologize if I was a bother."

"No worries at all. I'm happy to have answered your questions. Call us anytime. We're here to serve you."

Laurel disconnected the call. She should feel reassured. Her questions had been answered. Or had they?

CHAPTER THIRTEEN

Just as Laurel was leaving work for the day and about halfway across the school parking lot to her vehicle, her phone buzzed. She pulled out her phone from the bottom of her purse. She was surprised to see the name of the adoption agency.

"Hello," she answered tentatively, her hand painfully tight on the phone.

"Hello, Laurel," Mary Swindoll responded cheerfully. "And a very merry Christmas."

"The same to you." Laurel had no idea why Mary would be calling her out of the blue like this, and she was in a hurry to get home.

Mary didn't waste time getting to the purpose of her call. "Did Zach have a chance to talk to you about our website project?"

Zach? He'd heard from the adoption agency and not told her? He'd made no mention of it at all. Rather than appear in the dark, Laurel decided to play along. "I'm afraid not. We've both been so busy."

As always, Mary was gracious. "I totally understand. I had reached out to Zach because I thought the two of you would be the perfect couple for our website update, especially now that you've decided to renew your application."

The oxygen froze in Laurel's lungs, and for one crazy moment she found it impossible to breathe. Mary continued chatting on about the website redesign. A word or two made their way into Laurel's consciousness, but her heart remained stuck on the fact that Zach had gone behind her back and resubmitted their application, even after they'd agreed not to.

"I can understand how hard it's been after your last disappointment. I'm sure it wasn't an easy decision to reapply, and I applaud your courage."

"Yes . . ." Laurel managed to squeak out, sounding more like a rusty door hinge than anything human.

"How about I check with you after the first of the year?" Mary suggested. "That should give you and Zach time to decide if you're willing to be part of this project."

Laurel hadn't the wherewithal to respond. As it was, she found it nearly impossible to remain upright. She leaned against the side of her car for support.

"Would that work?" Mary asked when she didn't answer.

"Okay," she managed after several seconds passed.

Although she might have come across as being rude, Laurel cut off the call without a farewell. Her legs felt like they were about to go out from under her. Another few moments passed before Laurel was able to draw in a deep breath.

So that was it. That was the deep, dark secret her husband had been keeping from her. Laurel had accepted there would be no child for them.

But he hadn't. Even after their recent heart-to-heart conversations.

It became clear to Laurel in that moment her husband would never be able to accept the fact that she couldn't give him a family. To her face, he said he was content, but she knew better now. Zach had flat-out lied to her, and his betrayal cut sharper than any knife and penetrated deeper than any sword.

"Laurel," Britta Jackson called out as she walked toward Laurel in the parking lot. "Is everything all right?"

Unable to answer, Laurel stared blankly back at her fellow teacher as Britta hurriedly walked toward her.

"You've been standing by your car for a while now. I saw that you were on your phone. I hope it wasn't bad news."

Laurel tried to shake her head, but she couldn't force her neck to move. She noticed the slight bump of Britta's stomach. Not only was her teacher friend pregnant, but Laurel had heard that the latest ultrasound revealed that Britta and her husband were having twins. A boy and a girl. Yet Laurel couldn't even conceive one.

"I'm fine," she said, fearing Britta wouldn't accept her lie. "Have a good evening." With a sense of urgency, she climbed inside the car and started the engine. Unwilling to wait for the car to warm up, she barreled out of the parking lot, hitting the curb as she pulled onto the street.

Laurel had no memory of driving home. Only when she'd pulled into the short driveway did she realize she had traveled from the school to the house without remembering a single turn or street. Her hands were still white from clenching the steering wheel in a death grip as if it was the only thing in the world she had to hold on to. It took another minute for her limbs to cooperate enough to climb out of the vehicle and head into the house.

The warmth inside the entryway hit her like a fist, shocking her senses. She was grateful that no one was there to greet her, so she could have time to compose herself. What she'd learned had jarred her so badly that she was still struggling to breathe normally as she leaned against the closed door.

Laurel suddenly recalled the time when she was eight and had fallen off the tire swing she'd begged her father to hang from a tree branch in the backyard. The pain had been horrific, and she'd screamed for her mother, who had come running out of the house. Seeing Laurel's twisted arm, her mother had immediately called for an aid car, then held Laurel gently in her arms until the paramedics arrived. She could clearly hear her mother's voice in her head, even now, calmly and tenderly asking Laurel to take deep breaths, to manage the intense pain.

With her back still against the front door, Laurel employed her mother's words, drawing air deeply into her lungs and slowly releasing it, until she felt steady enough to move away from the door.

When she felt she could move, she forced a smile and stepped into the kitchen, looking for her grandmother and Mrs. Miracle, only to confirm that the quiet house was empty. She recalled that Mrs. Miracle and her nana were at the senior center for the annual Christmas dinner. That was something to be grateful for. She would be able to confront Zach without anyone else listening in on what was sure to be a difficult and painful conversation.

Laurel wandered aimlessly from one room to the next like a zombie, rubbing her hands together, a chill coming over her. Warm. Then cold. Then warm again. She'd had this same sensation two other times in her life: the day she'd broken her arm, and the day she'd been forced to surrender Jonathan. Her body didn't know how to respond to the intense pain that she had deep in her soul.

Hot tears burned on the rims of her eyes, but she refused to let them fall. With an aching heart, she found herself standing in front of the nursery. The door had remained shut since they'd been forced to hand Jonathan over to the caseworker. Laurel hadn't been able to bear going inside since then, as seeing it empty would only amplify the emptiness in her heart. That dreadful day had been the end for her. She knew she could endure no more, and Zach had

promised. Promised. He'd given his solemn word
that it was the end for him also . . . that it was time
to let go and accept that they weren't meant to be
parents.

She must have stood there for a good five minutes
before she realized the door to the nursery was ajar.
It was never left open. Someone must have gone inside. But why? And who?

Nana?

Her grandmother would have no reason to venture there. Nor Mrs. Miracle.

It had to be Zach.

Had he gone inside without her knowing? It
must have been recently—otherwise, she would
have noticed. But why would he enter this room of
hurt? Laurel tentatively pushed against the door
with just enough strength for it to slowly open.

A dark emptiness greeted her, and she sucked in
a gasp. How long she stood there staring into the
darkness, she couldn't answer. Her lungs hurt and
she realized she'd been holding her breath, which
she slowly released. Subconsciously, her arm reached
out to turn on the light. Instantly, light spilled into
the room. She found it just as she had left it.

The first thing her eyes fell on was the empty
rocking chair where she'd spent countless sleepless
nights rocking her tiny, struggling, drug-addicted
son, easing him through those first torturous months
of life. She looked over at the crib with the musical
mobile suspended above, which Jonathan had been
fascinated by. Even now she could picture him
stretching his tiny arms upward, so badly wanting

to reach the zoo animals that circled above his head. For just an instant, she almost smiled with the memory. That moment escaped quickly as she looked below the mobile at the empty crib. The crib that would always remain empty.

The changing table was stacked with disposable diapers. Jonathan had been quite the wiggler as she'd tried to change him or dress him. He'd twist and turn and reach for his toes, a challenge for Zach and Laurel, but they'd always be victorious, and happy to see Jonathan move and grow in the time they had with him.

Laurel blinked. The drawer was open. *What?* She knew for a fact that every drawer in that dresser had been tightly closed. Yet one was open only an inch or two—just enough for her to see a red bag. A red Macy's bag. In an instant, she knew exactly what was inside—the baby clothes Zach had promised to return.

Another broken promise. She could only guess at how many other promises her husband had broken.

Something else rested next to the shopping bag. With determined steps, she walked toward the dresser and opened it wide enough to find a box—a cigar box, of all things. She glared at it as if it were a poisonous snake that was prepared to strike and dig its fangs into her tender skin. She gingerly lifted the lid, and, seeing its contents, she leaped backward. If there was anything more to be discovered, she didn't have the heart to find out, and she quickly vacated the room, slamming the door behind her.

She checked the time and knew Zach was due

home any minute. Mentally, she prepared herself for the upcoming confrontation. In the past, it had been far too easy to ignore what should have been obvious. Laurel had to accept that she'd been willfully blind. All along, she suspected things weren't right between them. With school, worries about her nana, and the holiday program, it had been far too convenient to look the other way. To pretend.

She couldn't—wouldn't—turn blind eyes to this any longer.

Within a few minutes, Laurel heard the faint click of the front door opening and closing. Zach was home. She braced herself, drawing deep into her inner core for strength, readying herself to face him.

"Laurel?" Zach's voice echoed through the house.

With her hands folded primly in front of her, she stepped out from the hallway into the living room. Zach had removed his coat and hung it in the front closet.

He smiled when he turned to see her. "You just got home?" he asked, his smile warm and open. If he had been able to read her mood, it was clear he was deciding to ignore it. She recognized those signs, seeing how she'd often used the same avoidance tactic. Talking around a subject, looking to avoid any chance of a squabble or conflict—these strategies had become far too comfortable in their marriage.

She didn't answer until she noticed he was waiting for her response. "No . . . I've been here for a while now."

"Are you cold? Is the furnace acting up again?"

She blinked, finding his question odd. He must have read her puzzlement, because he grinned. "You're wearing your coat."

"Oh." She'd completely forgotten she had it on. Now that she thought about it, she had no idea where her purse was, either, and had to assume it remained in her car.

"Are you okay?" he asked, as she walked past him and went outside to retrieve her purse.

"I'm good," she said as she returned to the house, purse in hand.

"I know you're feeling the pressure of this holiday program."

"I said there isn't a problem." Her words were sharp, cold.

He continued to stare at her and apparently thought a change of subject might help. "Did you find time to call about Mrs. Miracle's references?"

"I did. Everything checked out."

"That's great." He continued to watch her every move.

Laurel could tell he was trying to gauge her mood. She went into the kitchen, needing to lean her back against the counter, for it seemed her knees were once again ready to fail her.

As she knew he would, Zach followed.

"I had a great day. The project I've been working on is coming together nicely." He paused, waiting for a response from her.

All Laurel was capable of was a simple, singular nod. The lump in her throat tightened, and for the

briefest of moments she was tempted to forget what
she'd discovered that afternoon. But she knew she
couldn't.

"I got a call after school," she managed to state,
without specifics.

Zach opened the refrigerator door and reached
for an apple. "What's for dinner?"

"I'd rather talk about the phone call."

"Okay. What was it about?" he said, taking a big
crunching bite of his apple. He seemed totally oblivi-
ous to what was about to happen.

"It was from Mary Swindoll."

The words fell between them like an explosion,
which, indeed, they were. Explosive. Zach's eyes
rounded, and he carefully, methodically, set the
apple down on the kitchen counter. His nonchalant
attitude was gone.

"Aren't you going to ask me what she had to
say?" She gestured toward him, indicating that she
looked for him to explain why she would receive a
cold call from the agency.

"She told you about the website?"

"Oh, she told me much more than that."

His Adam's apple bobbed up and down in his
throat as he swallowed a few times, realizing where
the conversation was going. He stuffed his hands
into the back pockets of his Dockers as Laurel continued.

"I'll admit that it came as a complete surprise to
learn that you'd gone behind my back and resubmitted our adoption application. Why, Zach? Why
would you do that? I'd told you that after losing

Jonathan, I couldn't do this anymore. I couldn't put my heart through that kind of torture ever again. And you agreed. Only recently, you told me . . ." The knot in her throat grew so fast it became impossible to finish the sentence.

"I know I should have told you. I . . . I thought . . . you know . . . I thought that we shouldn't close the door entirely. I figured that by not telling you what I'd done, that I was protecting you. Protecting your heart. If a baby *did* become available for adoption, then it would be a sweet surprise. I know how badly you wanted to be a mother, and I did it for you, Laurel. For us." He stretched out his arms as though pleading for her to understand, to believe he'd never do anything to intentionally hurt her.

"Don't kid yourself, Zach. It wasn't for *us*. You did it for *you*, for the dream of fatherhood, because of your *own* desires for a family."

"Laurel, that's not true."

She denied his words with a hard shake of her head. "After Jonathan, it was the end for me. You knew this. I told you this."

"I know, which is why—"

"You didn't return the baby clothes, did you? Don't bother to deny it. I found them in the dresser. And the cigars."

For an inkling of a second his eyes brightened. "The store wouldn't take the clothes back . . . I had the receipt and everything and the clerk said . . . Well, it doesn't matter now. I knew that if you discovered them you'd be upset, so I prayed and I asked God for

a sign . . . and then the cigars were from the gift exchange, and then I knew that God—"

Zach couldn't get his explanation out fast
enough.

"Zach, please. Stop. I can't bear to hear another
word."

His head sagged. "I don't know what you want
me to say. I'm sorry, Laurel. I never intended to hurt
you."

She believed that of him, but it didn't change the
bottom line. It didn't change what his actions had so
vividly spelled out to her in that moment of discov-
ery. A sky writer couldn't have made it any clearer.

"Zach, I know this isn't what you want to believe, but I need to say it. As much as I want to, I'll
never be able to give you a family. Those dreams we
shared that summer as we looked up into the sky
over Green Lake . . . I'm sorry, Zach." She paused
when her voice cracked. "I'm so sorry."

She took a moment before she was able to continue. "I gave it my all, but some of those dreams
weren't meant to be. You dreamed of having a family, and I can't give you one."

"But you are my family," Zach insisted.

"Apparently, I'm not enough," she said, jerking
her hands to her face and smearing the tears across
her cheeks.

"That's not true. You're more than enough.
You're all the family I want. You're all the family
that I need."

"Your actions speak otherwise, far louder than
your words."

"I love you, Laurel. You can't question that."

"I don't," she whispered back, struggling to contain her tears, although raging emotions were ripping through her like a hot knife. "Loving me isn't enough for you. You need more. You will always want more."

He lowered his eyes to the floor. "All I did was hang on to hope for us, Laurel. Yes, I put in our application. I was wrong to do it, and I was ready to withdraw it, but I asked God for a sign. That's when I got the cigars in the gift exchange at the office."

"And because of those cigars, you now believe?"

Eyes still downcast, he nodded. "I do. I believe. I honestly believe it's going to happen for us."

That was all Laurel needed to hear. Staring sightlessly into the distance, she remained frozen, and her breathing slowed, as did her pulse. It felt like the entire fabric of their marriage had been ripping apart, and this was the last thread. His words had convinced her beyond any arguing or reasoning that Zach would never be fulfilled in their marriage without a child.

"And that was why you brought both the baby clothes and the cigars to the house and hid them." Straightening her shoulders, she looked up so he would know the seriousness of what she was about to say. "I . . . I can't go on like this, Zach. I love you . . . I do. With everything I am, I love you. But I feel it would be best if I . . . if you found someone else."

He said nothing for several horrible seconds. "You don't mean that. You can't mean it."

Despite her grief, she knew in her heart it was the right thing to let him go. "I do, I really do."

They stood with only a few feet separating them, neither speaking. Zach's shoulders slumped in defeat. After what seemed like an eternity, he walked out of the room. Laurel heard the front door of the house open and close.

Shutting her eyes, she sank onto the floor, falling on her knees and weeping harder than she had in her life. Sobs racked her shoulders. Not only had she lost Jonathan, but along with that beautiful baby boy, her marriage was now gone. She finally had the courage to realize that she loved Zach enough to set him free, so he could have the wife and children he deserved.

How long she stayed on her knees, Laurel didn't know. She covered her face with both hands and wept for what seemed to be forever. When she heard the front door open, she sniffled and did her best to pull herself together to greet her grandmother and Mrs. Miracle.

CHAPTER FOURTEEN

Helen had no idea what had happened between Laurel and Zach. Mrs. Miracle had dropped her off after the Christmas dinner at the senior center; she was in high spirits, until she opened the door and caught sight of her granddaughter's ravaged face.

Laurel's eyes had been red and puffy, her skin blotchy. Before Helen could find out what was wrong, her granddaughter had rushed off to bed. Zach was nowhere to be found. Worry and concern kept Helen awake most of the night.

Come morning, when she heard Laurel in the kitchen, she tossed back her covers and climbed out of her warm bed. While she didn't want to pry, she needed to know what had happened between Laurel and Zach, for her own peace of mind, if nothing else.

Heading to the kitchen in her robe and slippers, Helen found her granddaughter leaning against the kitchen counter, her eyes closed, as if drawing deep inside herself for some inner strength.

"Laurel, my love. What is it?"

Laurel automatically moved into Helen's arms, as though she was desperately in need of consolation. She pressed her head on her grandmother's shoulder. Tears fell against Helen as her granddaughter spoke. "Zach . . . left."

"Left? He didn't come home last night? How long will he be gone?"

It was hard to make sense of Laurel's muffled reply. It sounded like she said "forever." That couldn't possibly be right. Zach loved Laurel. Helen never doubted his heartfelt love and affection for her granddaughter.

"He wants what I can't give him."

"Oh, Laurel . . ." Helen felt at a loss as to how best to comfort her precious granddaughter.

Laurel broke away from Helen, reaching for a tissue to blow her nose. Pure grit and determination marked her words as she sniffled and stated, "Today is the school program. I've got to get myself together."

"Oh dear," Helen whispered, pressing her fingers to her lips. "How will you manage?"

"I . . . I don't know, but I will. I have to. Everyone is counting on me." Reaching for a second tissue, she dabbed at her eyes and forced a weak smile.

"Have a cup of tea," Helen advised, hoping that would help calm her granddaughter's tender heart.

"You'll feel better." Yet she knew that no amount of makeup would disguise Laurel's ashen skin and red eyes.

"All the tea in China isn't going to fix this, Nana. I'll get through today the way I've survived everything else. I'm not your granddaughter for nothing." She kissed Helen on the cheek and bravely headed out the door.

Helen quickly dressed and ate her breakfast of tea and toast even before her companion arrived. She could hardly wait for Mrs. Miracle to show up so she could get an insight into what had gone so terribly wrong. For the next fifteen minutes, she was anxious. This was bad. Something needed to be done. Mrs. Miracle would know what to do, and if she couldn't count on an angel to intercede, then she didn't know what would happen.

"Oh my goodness. I'm so glad you're here," Helen burst out as soon as her companion entered the house.

"What is it?" Mrs. Miracle asked, removing her coat and scarf.

"It's Laurel and Zach," Helen anxiously explained. "Something's happened. I saw it on Laurel's face last night, then she broke down this morning when I asked her. Zach is gone and she said I shouldn't expect him back. I think I know the root of the problem," she said. "The door to the baby's bedroom was open."

"Ah yes," Mrs. Miracle returned in a soothing voice. "I know all about that. Nothing to worry yourself over, my dear."

"I don't think you understand the seriousness of the situation," Helen said. "Did you hear me when I said Zach wasn't coming home?"

Mrs. Miracle went about pouring herself a cup of tea, apparently unconcerned. "I heard."

"And today, of all days, is the school program."

"Yes. All will be well. Helen, you need to trust," she gently replied, as she tenderly patted Helen's hand.

Mrs. Miracle's calm reassurances were exactly what she needed to hear. From the moment Helen had stepped into the kitchen and found her granddaughter an emotional mess, her heart had been racing like a fire engine, speeding to a blaze.

"Relax, now, and join me with a cup of tea. Before you know it, it'll be time to leave for the school."

"But will Laurel be okay? And Zach?"

"They will, I promise."

Helen sipped her tea and took Mrs. Miracle at her word.

The two spent the remainder of the day knitting and chatting together until it was time to head to the school for the afternoon program. All Helen could do was pray that Laurel had pulled herself together to see all of her hard work come to life for what was the biggest event of the school year.

By the time Helen and Mrs. Miracle reached the school, it was abuzz with activity. Cars flooded the small parking lot, spilling onto the side streets surrounding the building. Parents and grandparents crowded the large space that served as an auditorium as well as a gym and a cafeteria. Neat, orderly rows of folding chairs had been set in place, facing the stage. Both sides had several small potted live Christmas trees of varying heights, strung with lights and handmade ornaments. Student artwork, all with holiday themes, was clipped on clotheslines along the remaining sides of the large gathering space.

Helen watched as each grade paraded out in single file, to the delight of their families. Mrs. Miracle sat in the chair next to her. The older woman on her other side clasped her hands together in delight as she stretched one way and then another, attempting to find the child she had come to see.

Leaning over to Helen, the woman whispered excitedly, "That's my granddaughter."

"Which one?" Helen asked.

"The second-grader in the red dress."

Several of the girls in line wore the same color dress. But Helen smiled back and whispered, "She's adorable."

Such proud parents and grandparents, all around her.

"That's *my* granddaughter," Helen said, leaning back to the other grandmother and pointing to Laurel. She was grateful to see that all traces of Laurel's emotional breakdown were erased from her face. How Laurel had managed to pull herself together, she could only speculate. "She's the first-grade teacher," Helen added.

"Mrs. McCullough? I recognize her. My granddaughter had her last year. She's a wonderful teacher. My daughter was the homeroom parent for her class, and she said all the children loved her."

"Yes, she's a special young woman," Helen said proudly.

The program was about to start, and the room quieted as the principal, Mr. Adams, stood to welcome the audience with a content look on his face at the high rate of attendance.

"First, I want to say how pleased we are here at Ronald Reagan Elementary to welcome the families of our students," he began. "The students and staff have worked hard to put together this holiday program. I want to especially thank Mrs. McCullough for overseeing this entire event. Please turn off your cellphones so the children's hard work can be our primary focus this afternoon. Without further delay," Mr. Adams declared, "let the show begin!"

Helen silently said a prayer for Laurel and the children. Laurel had worked hard, putting in a copious amount of her own time to bring the talents of each class together so that every student participated in one way or another.

Applause erupted. Helen clapped loudly, stretching her neck to get a better view of Laurel's first-grade class standing to the side of the stage, antsy and anxious for their turn. The kindergarteners performed first. When they had finished to thunderous appreciation, Laurel's class marched onto the platform. The children waited for her signal to begin singing. Their sweet, young voices echoed through the room. Several parents crouched in the aisles, waiting their turn to take pictures. The flashes of the cellphones lit up the children's faces. Others held up their phones from their seats, recording the heavenly sound. Helen imagined that this was what young angels-in-training must sound like. She knew Laurel would be pleased with how well they did.

One of the highlights of the program for Helen was listening to the school band, which was the grand finale. Laurel had told her how hard the children had worked on the instrumental portion. She leaned forward as the band teacher raised the baton and the children started to play. There were a few squeaks from the trumpet players, and one violinist was a few beats behind the others. The boy playing the tuba was smaller than his instrument. How he managed to hold on and play was a marvel, and Helen had to give him credit.

After several bars, the grandmother next to her moved closer and inquired, "Can you tell what song they're playing?"

"It's 'O Christmas Tree,' I believe," Helen whispered back. It did take some imagination to make out the familiar Christmas carol.

"Right." She bobbed her head with the last portion of the song, chasing the melody.

The song finished and the band members proudly stood and bowed to the audience, who came to their feet in a standing ovation. Mrs. Miracle clapped loudly with delight. Helen couldn't have been prouder of Laurel. Her granddaughter had put her whole heart into this program, from beginning to end.

Because it was the last day of school before the winter break, the children were dismissed to their parents at the end of the show, starting with the youngest grades. Mrs. Miracle told Helen she'd meet her at the back of the auditorium.

Helen watched as several parents stepped forward to speak to Laurel, thank her, and exchange holiday greetings. She waited patiently for her turn. It was important that Laurel knew she was there.

"Nana," Laurel said when she saw her grandmother. For a fraction of a second, her smile faltered before she hugged Helen.

"You did an amazing job," Helen said, and had rarely been prouder of her granddaughter, especially under the circumstances.

"Thank you, Nana."

Helen could hear the exhaustion in her voice. "Oh, Laurel, it was wonderful. Simply perfect. The children were amazing. *You're* amazing."

Laurel gave her another loving squeeze. "Thanks, Nana. I'm glad you were here."

Helen understood the underlying message. She knew Zach had taken time off to go, and how pleased Laurel had been that he could attend. But Zach hadn't showed. Helen's heart broke for her granddaughter.

"Oh, sweetheart," she whispered, wanting desperately to reassure Laurel. "Everything will work out the way God intends. Just you wait and see."

A young girl—the second-grader in the red dress

that the grandmother next to Helen had pointed out—hurried over to her former teacher. "Mrs. McCullough! Mrs. McCullough!" she said, yanking on Laurel's sleeve.

Breaking eye contact with Helen, Laurel focused her attention on the child. "Yes, Bella. What is it?" She crouched down so she was eye level with the youngster.

The girl smiled and blinked several times. "I want you to know you're going to be a really good mommy."

Helen watched as the color drained from her granddaughter's face. "Thank you, Bella." Laurel's cheeks quivered with a forced smile.

Helen noticed the effort it took for Laurel to blink back tears.

"My mommy thinks so, too."

At what cost, Helen could only speculate, but Laurel managed to give a gracious reply and gently hugged the child.

"Okay. I have to go now," Bella said, breaking away from Laurel. "Merry Christmas!"

"The same to you, Bella."

Helen watched as the girl scooted across the auditorium floor and back to her mother. Bella's mother gave Laurel a small wave before tucking her arm around her daughter's shoulders and leading her out of the room.

"I had Bella in first grade," Laurel told her grandmother. "She's a sweet, good-natured child, and her mom was a wonderful homeroom parent. It's a lovely family."

Mrs. Miracle joined them and complimented Laurel. "You did a fine job."

"Thank you," she whispered.

Reaching out, Mrs. Miracle gently squeezed Laurel's forearm. "Trust," she whispered.

Laurel's returning smile was forced. "I'll see you both at home."

"Don't be long," Helen said.

"I won't be," she promised.

From the forlorn look about her, Helen knew home was the one place her granddaughter needed right now, above all else. As Laurel had done as a ten-year-old girl, she would go to the place where she could find the comfort and the security that her heart needed.

CHAPTER FIFTEEN

Laurel stayed behind to be sure the auditorium/gymnasium was cleared and put back in order. The maintenance staff was busy taking down the folding chairs when Laurel turned and saw Zach standing in the back with his hands in his pockets, studying her.

She stood, frozen in place. A wrecking ball couldn't have moved her. She was certain all the blood in her body had stopped flowing.

For what felt like an eternity, all they did was stare at each other.

It was Zach who moved first, walking toward her in slow, deliberate steps. He didn't look any better than she felt. His clothes were rumpled and his hair askew.

"Hey," he said, his voice low and tight. His eyes locked on her.

Unable to speak, she nodded in return.

"You did good. The program was great."

"You were here?"

He nodded. "Last row, behind the tuba player's mother," he said, one side of his mouth tilted upward in a half-smile. "I said I'd come, didn't I?"

So that was it. He was fulfilling a promise. She squared her shoulders. "I need to get home."

"Can you spare the time for a cup of coffee?" he asked.

Oh, how she was tempted. Her shattered heart leaned toward him as though drawn by a magnet. Everything in her wanted to say yes, but she couldn't. He'd made the decision when he walked out the door and didn't return. Laurel knew she'd need a clean break, otherwise that door would become a revolving one. She had to be strong. "I . . . I don't think . . ."

"Please?"

That lone word was her undoing. All her resolve melted as her heart caved in. "Okay."

Because there's a Starbucks on nearly every corner in Seattle, they decided to meet there in the next fifteen minutes.

Zach got there first, and by the time she arrived, he was at the counter, ordering their drinks. Laurel found them a table by the window. Almost instantly, Zach returned with two drinks.

"I got you a peppermint latte," he said. "Your favorite."

"Thank you." She looked down at the drink rather than meet his gaze.

"My guess is you went without anything to eat this morning."

Her stomach wouldn't tolerate food and he knew it.

Silence stretched like a summertime taffy pulled between them, rough and sticky. Zach was the one who'd asked her for coffee, and so she waited for him to speak first.

"I drove around most of the night," he said, his voice hoarse and full of emotion. "That gave me plenty of opportunity to think about what you said. Did you mean it, Laurel? Were you sincere in saying you wanted me to find a wife who could give me a family?"

She sipped her latte before she replied. "Yes. I meant it." Even now, after all these hours, she could tell that he still had trouble believing her.

Zach leaned back in the chair and ran his hand over his face. "Don't you know by now that I don't want anyone but you?"

"Please," she whispered, her voice so faint she couldn't be sure he heard her. "Please don't make this any more difficult than it already is."

"Don't you understand? What more do I need to say to convince you that you're far more than my wife? You're my best friend, my entire life. I don't know how you can even think you're not enough for me, when you are my whole world."

She raised her head and met his eyes. His look was dark and intense, pleading.

"I don't want to live if it isn't with you. Please, Laurel. Don't let my mistakes destroy us. I couldn't bear it. Please forgive me. We can make this work."

Laurel, in all honesty, wasn't sure she could bear

life without him, either. Tears flooded her eyes and rained down her cheeks.

"Baby, please don't cry. It hurts me to see you like this. If you can't forgive me . . ."

"Are you absolutely sure, Zach? I can't go through another night like that again."

"I'm one hundred percent sure." He stood so fast that he nearly toppled his chair over. He reached for her, pulling her off the seat and into his arms. Laurel was immediately wrapped in his embrace. His hug was tight enough to cut off her breath.

Standing in Starbucks, they clung to each other. "I'm sure, too," she managed to choke out from behind the tears that had begun to flow again.

"We're a team, Laurel. We're a family—you and me. Not having a baby won't change what we have between us. We were meant to be together and I won't let you send me away."

That was what she needed to know. It was enough. It was more than enough.

"Excuse me." A woman's voice broke through the fog of their reunion. "Are you finished with this table?"

"It's all yours." And with his arm tucked around Laurel's waist, he added, "My wife and I are heading home."

"You'll come to the Christmas Eve service with us, won't you?" Helen asked Mrs. Miracle as they said their good-byes. This was Mrs. Miracle's last day before Christmas. She would miss the woman who had become a dear friend, but it would be hard to justify the expense of a paid companion when it wasn't necessary. As compensation, two uninterrupted weeks with Laurel would be exactly what her heart needed to prepare her for the holidays.

"I'll meet you at the church with bells on," Mrs. Miracle assured, and in a low voice only Helen could hear, she added, "And I mean literally. You'll hear me before you see me. Listen for the bells."

Laurel had gone into the other room, so Helen felt free to speak, although quietly. "I'll keep my ears open. Can you tell me when to expect the baby's arrival?"

The angel's smile was huge. "Soon."

"Before Christmas?"

"I can't be sure, but if not before, then shortly thereafter."

"That's wonderful news." Helen was relieved. As tempting as it was, she hadn't said anything to Laurel or Zach. Something had changed between the young couple. Helen didn't fully understand what had transpired the day of the school production, but soon after the performance, Laurel had returned to the house with Zach. Helen had wept quiet tears of joy to see the two reunited. She decided she didn't need an explanation, as long as they were back together again.

After that point, the two seemed more in love than ever, exchanging tender looks and kisses. Helen noticed the way they made excuses to be close to each other, to hold hands, and to give each other tender, loving touches. Whatever had happened between Laurel and Zach had united them in a way she hadn't noticed since the early years of their courtship and marriage.

"So, it's a date. I'll meet you at the church for the Christmas Eve service," Mrs. Miracle confirmed. She looked over her shoulder to make sure Laurel remained in the kitchen. "And, Helen? I just wanted you to know that Shirley, Goodness, and Mercy will be joining me."

"That's wonderful." Helen couldn't be more pleased, but then again, she wasn't sure she'd recognize them. She almost felt she knew the trio of angels, from everything her friend had shared about her special friends. "Will they be arriving in human form . . . you know, like normal people?"

"Not all of them."

This was a puzzling statement. "How will I know who they are?"

"Let me clarify," Mrs. Miracle added indulgently. "You may not see all of them with your eyes, but you'll hear them."

"I'll hear them?" Again, Helen found that perplexing, wondering if they would have bells on, too. "Will they jingle?"

Mrs. Miracle laughed loud enough for Laurel to stick her head out of the kitchen to see what was going on. "What's so funny, you two?" she asked.

"Your grandmother."

"Mrs. Miracle," Helen exclaimed at the same time.

Laurel grinned and returned to preparing lunch.

Her companion waited until Laurel was out of sight again before adding, "They'll be singing with the choir, but only one will be visible to the human eye. They love helping choirs out, especially during this time of the year. Afterward, I enjoy listening to the congregation's comments on the way out of the church. It amuses me every time. People say the craziest things."

"Oh?"

"Things like 'The choir has never sounded so good.' Well, it's no wonder, right?"

"Right," Helen agreed.

"Another of my favorites is when someone declares that the choir sounded like it was made up of angels. And then there's the pessimist, who always finds fault, no matter what. You'll hear that person saying, 'It's a shame the choir doesn't sound that good every week.'"

Helen cupped her mouth to smother her laugh. She'd met gloomy people like that over the years—those who always looked at the glass as half-empty, no matter how big the glass, or how full it was already.

"Do you sing?" Helen asked.

"Some," Mrs. Miracle admitted, "but not much. God gave me other talents."

"There's singing in heaven, isn't there?" Helen could only imagine how beautiful it must sound.

"Oh yes, but the music is out of this world. You can't compare it to what you hear on earth. There's no possible way to describe heaven's music."

"I'll hear it myself one day."

Mrs. Miracle placed her hand over Helen's and gave it a gentle squeeze, "Yes, you will."

After saying her good-byes, Mrs. Miracle collected her coat and purse and left the house. Helen took a short catnap in her favorite chair while Laurel remained in the kitchen. The next thing she knew, Laurel was bringing her lunch.

"I made your recipe for beef barley soup," she said, setting a bowl on the television tray in front of Helen.

"I didn't mean to sleep so long, and I don't like you waiting on me like this," she protested. "I can come to the table."

"Stay right where you are," Laurel insisted. "I know Mrs. Miracle served you lunch every day. I can do the same."

"Then you need to sit and join me, just as she did. If it's all right, I think I'll head over to the senior center this afternoon. Today is bingo and I'm feeling lucky."

"Of course. I'll walk over with you." Laurel brought out a second television tray and sat next to Helen with her own lunch. She blew on the spoon to cool down the hot soup. "You're going to miss Mrs. Miracle, aren't you?"

"I am," Helen admitted. "She hasn't been with me for long, but she has had a strong impact on us all."

"Yes, she has," Laurel agreed, smiling.

———

Laurel walked the short three blocks to the senior center with her grandmother. When they entered the facility, Helen was greeted by three men, who all vied to be the one to pull out her chair at the long table set with the bingo cards. Helen found it amusing. Laurel observed her grandmother with a new set of eyes—she truly was an attractive woman.

"Your grandmother has been turning heads ever since she set foot in the center," a woman commented, coming over to greet Laurel. "I'm Mary Lou. I used to live three houses down the street from where you live now. Your mother, Kelly, and my Julie used to play together as children. We moved when the girls started high school."

Laurel smiled indulgently, pleased that her grandmother had reconnected with her friend.

"I was happy to find Helen coming to the center. It's been so good getting reacquainted with her."

"I'm pleased to meet you," Laurel said, glancing around the room, which was filling with seniors carting their bingo gear. This was apparently a hot game.

Mary Lou offered to drop Helen back at the house following bingo, so after a few minutes to make sure Nana had settled in with her friend, Laurel returned home.

There would be no tubs of licorice for Helen today, as Lady Luck wasn't on her side. She and Mary Lou chatted all the way home. Mary Lou promised to collect her after the holidays were over for the

Zumba class being held every Monday morning at the senior center.

That night, Helen's dreams had been full of Robert. As she slowly awoke in the morning, she clung to remnants of the dream, letting them linger. How she missed her husband. He'd always made Christmas special for her, decorating the outside of the house with a multitude of lights. Helen had loved how they brightened the house, and how, in the darkest part of winter, the lights cheered her and brought her joy. Robert knew that and was willing to put in long hours in the cold, climbing up and down the ladder, stringing lights around their roofline and all of the outside trees, because he loved his wife.

When it came to gift-giving, Robert had sincerely tried to find something special that he knew would please her, even when their budget was tight. Helen had never complained when he'd chosen household appliances as gifts instead of something more personal. The real gift, in Helen's mind, was his love and those outside lights.

This was the same love she now saw flowing between Zach and Laurel. No matter what the future held, she knew that it would be with them as it had been with her and Robert, the man who had been her soulmate, the love of her life.

Helen joined the young couple for breakfast, and she felt she needed to let Zach know that she'd invited her home companion to the upcoming Christmas Eve candlelight service.

"I hope you don't care that she'll be joining us."

"Why would I? Mrs. Miracle is more than welcome."

Reaching for a slice of toast, Helen kept her eyes lowered to hide a smile. "I understand the choir is in tip-top shape, rehearsing their hearts out. We bumped into one of the ladies from church on our walk the other day, and she said the choir had never sounded better."

"Really?" Laurel replied. "The last I heard, Mrs. Nelson was desperately searching for additional altos. Mrs. Murphy is joining her children in New York for the holidays, and both Alice Knight and Brenda Nichols have that awful flu bug that's going around." Their neighborhood church choir was small, and a few missing voices could make a world of difference.

"Someone must have stepped in," Zach said. "I always look forward to the music on Christmas Eve."

"Last Sunday, Pastor Warren announced that a trumpet player would be playing at the Christmas Eve service," Laurel added.

Helen could almost hear the triumphant sound now. There was nothing like the sound of a trumpet accompanying the choir to her favorite Christmas carol, "Joy to the World." It gave her chills just thinking about it.

That evening after dinner, the three settled in front of the television for a Hallmark Christmas movie. Helen watched as Laurel and Zach snuggled together. It seemed the two couldn't get close enough. It made her think back to when she and Robert were young, and it gladdened her heart. She continued to knit the baby blanket. A sense of urgency had filled her, as Mrs. Miracle said Laurel's baby would be arriving anytime now. With every available minute, she'd picked up her needles. She ended the row and held it up to gauge the size.

"What knitting project are you starting, Nana? It looks like the beginning of a blanket. I love the shade of pink."

Helen instantly knew what a deer caught in the headlights of a car must feel like. She didn't want to lie, and yet she didn't want to mention anything about the baby, either.

"Thank you," she said, after a brief pause, rationing her words and deciding to leave it at that. Laurel believed that her grandmother was at the start of a project, but little did she know Helen was nearing the end. The small, soft blanket would be perfect to bring the baby home from the hospital in.

Helen stayed up much later than usual, through the end of the romantic comedy. She'd finished the repeat of the last pattern on the blanket and bound off the last stitches. All that was needed now was to block the soft blanket. Then it would be ready for the baby's arrival.

Oh, what a lovely surprise this infant would be for Laurel and Zach. The precious baby would be coming into a home full of love, with parents who would treasure her as the gift from God that she was.

CHAPTER SIXTEEN

Christmas Eve arrived as a clear and bright winter day. After school had let out for the holiday break, Laurel and her grandmother had finished baking cookies with the dough that Mrs. Miracle had helped Nana prepare ahead of time.

Early that morning, the two women had worked to plate and wrap and put bows on the platters of Christmas cookies. Nana missed the cheerful presence of her companion, and worried that her friend might forget the church service scheduled for that evening. She talked about Mrs. Miracle nonstop, sharing memories of their fun times together, their excursion at the Pike Place Market, and their afternoon walks.

When they finished packaging the holiday treats, Laurel headed out to distribute the platters to the next-door neighbors and the staff at the church office as well as to the post office. Nana had taught her the importance of recognizing and thanking those who gave of themselves to others.

Laurel spent the latter part of the morning at a crowded grocery store. She hadn't expected it to be so jam-packed, and it took far longer than she would have liked to get through the maze of shoppers.

When she returned home, she found her grandmother busy in the kitchen, making homemade cinnamon rolls for Christmas morning. It'd been two or three years since Nana had gone to the trouble of baking sweet rolls. It did wonders for Laurel to see her grandmother active and happy again. With her relationship with Zach squared away, she knew this was going to be a special Christmas.

After unpacking the groceries, Laurel turned on some Christmas music, and the two women put together the traditional side dishes to cook for their Christmas dinner. They prepared the baked-potato casserole and the green-bean side dish, and then mixed the spices for the rib roast. This was the traditional Christmas dinner that Nana served every year.

When the last dish was prepped, Laurel and Nana looked around and sighed at the state of the kitchen. The sink was full of pots and pans and an assortment of dirty utensils and prep tools. Three to four cookbooks were open and spread across the kitchen counter. It looked like the contents of half the spice cabinet were scattered in every nook and cranny.

"Wow," Zach said, standing in the doorway leading into the room, "it looks like a bomb went off in here."

"We know," Laurel said, hugging her husband around the waist. "It's been that kind of day. Nana and I have been busy since the minute you left this morning. We're grateful you're home earlier than usual, so you can help with the cleanup."

With the three working together, the kitchen was back to normal in short order. Dinner was a quick affair, as they needed to leave for the Christmas Eve service. By six-thirty, they were ready to head out the door. Zach had helped Nana into the car and closed the door when his phone chirped. He quickly glanced down, frowned, and turned his phone to silent.

"Who was that?" Laurel asked, standing outside the passenger side of their car.

"Mary Swindoll. I left a message for her a few days ago. She must be getting back to me now."

Laurel knew why he'd reached out to Mary. He was withdrawing their application.

"I'll return her call next week," he said, and shoved his phone into his back pocket. They climbed into the car and gave each other a warm embrace.

"Listen, you two—if we don't get going," Helen interrupted, "we'll be late for church. You know how busy it gets on Christmas Eve, and I don't think you want to park a half-mile away."

"There's always plenty of parking, Nana," Laurel said gently.

Nana was right. By the time they arrived at the

church, Zach got one of the last parking spots in the lot.

"Do you see Mrs. Miracle?" Helen asked, scanning the inside of the church as they sought out a pew. "We have to save a spot for her."

"I don't see her yet," Laurel said.

"She should be here by now."

"She might have forgotten, Nana. Don't get your hopes up."

"Mrs. Miracle will be here," Helen assured her. "She's a woman of her word. I've never known her to be late, though," she added, looking concerned.

Zach escorted them into the pew and the three sat down. Laurel noticed that her grandmother saved a spot next to her and kept fidgeting, looking over her shoulder several times.

"Nana, didn't you just get done telling me Mrs. Miracle would be here? Stop worrying."

Her grandmother immediately settled down. "You're right. There's no need for me to fuss."

At that very moment, Laurel heard the distant harmony of tinkling bells. Nana straightened and looked over her shoulder again, knowing that they were all now in the company of special guests.

"You hear that, too?" she asked Nana. It was odd that no one around them seemed to notice.

"Yes!" Her grandmother smiled, seeming to hold back a secret. "I know you'll find this hard to believe, but it's the angels arriving."

"The angels," Laurel repeated skeptically.

"It's Mrs. Miracle's closest friends arriving— Shirley, Goodness, and Mercy." Her grandmother turned completely around to look down the center aisle. It did seem that the sound of bells came from the back of the church and was growing more distinct.

"Mrs. Miracle told me three of her closest friends would be attending this evening." She lowered her voice to a soft whisper. "They are angels, too."

Laurel hid her amusement as best she could.

"She said I'd know when they arrived when I heard the bells. What I didn't know was that you'd hear them, too."

Laurel looked to Zach and whispered, "Do you hear bells?"

He looked up from his program with an inquisitive look and signaled that he did with a nod.

The woman on the other side of Zach leaned over. "I don't hear a thing. What's all this talk about bells?"

Laurel didn't know what to tell the woman who had clearly made it a point to listen to their conversation, so she repeated what Nana had explained to her. "My grandmother says that the angels have arrived."

The woman's facial expression suggested that she thought they were a bunch of loonies. She scrunched a few more inches away from them in the pew and returned to minding her own business.

The service was just about to start when, sure enough, Mrs. Miracle arrived, looking a bit breathless. She scooted past several others in the pew to sit next to Helen. She whispered something to Nana, who clapped her hand over her mouth to hide her sharp burst of laughter.

Laurel didn't know what was so funny but decided not to ask. Instead, she focused her attention to the front of the church, where the choir members were walking in single file, dressed in their long, dark blue robes. It was a small group of about a dozen members.

"Laurel," Zach whispered, squeezing her arm. His mouth sagged open.

"What is it?"

"That woman in the choir . . . the third one on the left in the front row. Do you know her?"

"No. I don't think I've seen her before. Why?"

Zach lowered his voice. "She's the salesclerk who sold me all those baby clothes—the ones that I couldn't return. What is *she* doing here?"

"Honey, it's church. And it's Christmas Eve. Everyone's welcome."

"Of course everyone is welcome, but don't you think it's highly unusual this woman—someone I'd never seen until my strange experience at Macy's—that this same person would show up at the Christmas Eve service, in the choir, acting like she was a long-standing member?"

"Zach, honestly—you're making more of this than you should. I'm sure I told you about the choir seeking out replacements due to the flu going around."

"Yes, but still . . . what are the chances?"

Their conversation was interrupted when Pastor Warren stepped forward and spoke a few words of welcome, then asked everyone to stand for the opening hymn of "Silent Night," to be sung by the congregation and the choir.

Zach and Laurel shared a hymnal. The piano player's fingers moved skillfully over the keys with the few opening bars of the introduction. As soon as the choir started to sing, Laurel snapped her mouth closed. Although few in number, the choir sounded as big and bold as one five times as large. They made—she hated to use the cliché—a heavenly sound. Even Pastor Warren was taken by surprise. He looked over his shoulder at the small group behind him, his eyes wide with wonder at the glorious harmony.

Helen and Mrs. Miracle sat for the next hymn while most of the congregation stood. When Laurel turned around to check on her grandmother, she found the two women with their heads together, whispering animatedly. She was tempted to hush them as she would noisy, misbehaving children in her class. What a reversal that would've been— Laurel chastising her grandmother about proper behavior in church.

The congregation sat for a brief sermon about the birth of the Christ Child. The highlight was the story of the angels who visited the shepherds, heralding the good news of peace on earth and goodwill toward mankind with the arrival of the Christ Child. Zach and Laurel both noticed that while Pastor Warren was speaking, the woman from the department store squirmed in her seat, with an expression on her face like a first-grader who wanted to share a show-and-tell item with the rest of the class. She seemed to have a burning desire to supplement the pastor's sermon. It was almost comical to watch.

Following the sermon, the choir stood to sing "Hark! The Herald Angels Sing," after the trumpeter had performed the prelude. Again, Laurel was amazed at how beautifully the choir's voices blended together. She'd attended this same church from the time she was ten years old, but she'd never heard the choir sound this good.

Zach leaned over to comment in her ear. "Incredible."

Halfway through the song, Zach's phone buzzed in his pocket. He didn't bother to look at who it was.

After the traditional lighting of the candles, the choir sang two additional Christmas carols. The evening ended with one congregational carol before the pastor closed with an evening prayer.

As they left the church, several people made it a point to stop and wish Helen a merry Christmas, as they hadn't seen her in church much in the last few months. Helen's eyes were bright as she walked down the church steps with Mrs. Miracle. The two were arm in arm when Nana turned to Zach.

"Did you see her?"

"See who?"

"Mercy."

"Who's Mercy?" Zach asked.

Mrs. Miracle intervened. "You ran into Mercy while Christmas shopping recently."

A nerve twitched in Zach's cheek. "The sales-clerk at Macy's? Her name is Mercy? As far as I'm concerned, that woman has a lot to answer for, after all the trouble she caused me."

Mrs. Miracle appeared not to hear Zach, but Nana quickly added, "Shirley was there, too, only you couldn't see her. And Goodness, too."

The conversation was interrupted by Zach's phone humming again in his pocket. He sighed with frustration.

"What is it with people? Don't they know that it's Christmas Eve, and that most people are spending time with their families?"

"I believe it would be in your best interest to answer this time, Zach," Mrs. Miracle told him.

He glanced at the number and exhaled sharply. "It's Mary Swindoll, and this is the third time she's called. This is not a night to be making business calls."

"For the love of heaven," Helen snapped. "Answer the blasted phone."

Laurel was appalled. Her grandmother had never been so sharp with Zach. Or with her, for that matter.

"All right, all right."

Zach placed the phone next to his ear. "Yes, Mary," he said. "I apologize for not answering sooner. I was in church at our Christmas Eve service. I called you earlier in the week to . . ." He stopped and glanced over at Laurel, swallowed hard, and blinked.

Laurel placed her hand on his forearm, wondering at the change in her husband, who'd grown quiet and serious.

"What is it?" she asked.

"Now?" Zach said, speaking into the phone, although he barely sounded like himself. "Tonight? But we . . . Of course. Yes, yes, but I'll need to talk to Laurel." He turned his back and continued talking, nodding like he expected the person on the other line to see.

Laurel did her best to listen in, but a few acquaintances stopped to chat while she was straining to hear her husband. She made polite conversation, which made it impossible to decipher the purpose of Mary Swindoll's persistence.

Desperate to find out what it was all about, Laurel turned to Mrs. Miracle after the people left. "Do *you* know what's going on?"

"Zach will tell you in a couple of minutes," Nana jumped in to explain, gently patting the sleeve of Laurel's thick winter coat. "All is well. There's nothing for you to worry about. Not a single thing."

Everyone else seemed to be aware of what was happening, but not Laurel. "I heard Zach mention a hospital," she said.

"Patience," Mrs. Miracle whispered.

By this time the church parking lot had nearly emptied and the four of them were the only ones left standing near their car.

Finally, after what seemed like a lifetime, Zach lowered the phone and turned to Laurel.

"What is it?" she asked, her eyes searching his for answers.

After what seemed an interminable amount of time, Zach did nothing but look at her, his heart in his eyes. "It's Mary Swindoll. She's at the hospital, where a young mother has chosen us to adopt her baby."

Laurel's hand flew to her heart as if she needed to hold it in place. "A baby . . . There's a baby for *us*?"

Zach's glistening eyes revealed the depth of his emotion. "The choice is yours, Laurel. Like I told you before, baby or no baby, you're all the family I need."

"Of course we want the baby," she cried.

Immediately Zach brought the phone back to his ear and told Mary, "We're on our way." Then, grabbing hold of Laurel's hand, he added, "The mother is in labor and wants us to come to the hospital."

Laurel felt like her knees were about to buckle.

Seeing her shock, Zach placed his arm around her waist and helped her remain upright.

"But we . . . we aren't prepared for a baby."

"But we are. Those baby clothes, remember them? The bag we'd decided to donate to charity after the holidays?" He was laughing and nearly crying, both at once. Laurel laughed, too, as tears of joy flooded her own eyes.

Mrs. Miracle stepped forward and waved her hand, attracting their attention. "I believe you'll have plenty of time to get whatever else you will need before you bring your daughter home."

"Our daughter?" Laurel and Zach said in unison. "How do you know we're having a daughter?"

"My goodness. You people!" Nana exclaimed, tossing her arms in the air. "Mrs. Miracle told me about the baby the first day she arrived. I've kept it a secret all this time. Didn't I tell you we had a Caring Angel? A real one? Now scoot, you two—and get to the hospital!"

CHAPTER SEVENTEEN

After dropping Nana and Mrs. Miracle off at the house, Laurel and Zach raced to the hospital. Laurel was dumbstruck as Zach pulled into a parking space. Together they raced toward the double-wide glass doors.

Laurel came to a screeching halt when she saw that the receptionist space was empty. She had no clue where they were supposed to go. Her heart slammed against her ribs and she froze. She was terrified and exhilarated at the same time. This had to be a dream. It must be. Soon she'd wake up and find this had been only a figment of her imagination.

"Third floor! The elevators are this way!" Zach shouted, grabbing hold of her hand, jerking her forward to the point that she stumbled behind him.

Is this real? Could it possibly be happening?

By the time they reached the elevators, they were both out of breath. It seemed to take an interminable amount of time for the elevator to move, and for the sluggish doors to open. When it did, they entered and collapsed against the back wall, panting and excited.

Laurel placed her hand over her heart to find it beating frantically. "I can't believe this is happening."

"I can't, either."

When the doors opened on the third floor, they leaped out, paused, looking to the left and to the right, not knowing which direction to go. Anticipating their arrival, Mary Swindoll appeared from around the corner.

"Mary, we're here!" Zach proclaimed.

She greeted them with a big smile. "I can see that. Let's sit down for a minute and I'll fill you in." She led them to a quiet corner in a nearby waiting room. Laurel and Zach sat on the sofa. Zach reached for Laurel's hand.

Mary took the chair and sat close to the edge of the cushion, angling so her knees nearly touched Laurel's. "Zach, if you recall when we spoke last week, I mentioned the high school girl who'd decided to place her baby for adoption."

Laurel looked at her husband. Zach hadn't said anything about this.

Sensing her confusion, he glanced at her. "I asked about any babies coming up for adoption, and Mary told me there was a teenager who was working with another caseworker. She said the girl had already chosen the adoptive family."

"It appears that this family knows you, Laurel."

"The girl and her family know *me*?" she asked, folding her hands over her heart.

"Apparently so," Mary confirmed. "The family name is Bancroft."

Zach shook his head, indicating that the name didn't mean anything to him. He looked to Laurel. "What about you? Is the name familiar?"

The scene after the recent school holiday program suddenly played back in Laurel's head. Tears gathered in her eyes. "Bella," she whispered.

"Bella?"

"She was in my first-grade class last year. Isabella Bancroft."

"But how does this all connect back to you?"

"It must be her older sister. I'd met her during the school year. A smart, beautiful girl."

"You're right, Laurel. Her name is Lizzy," Mary supplied. "She's a high school senior, and Isabella is her youngest sister."

Laurel squeezed Zach's hand. "This totally explains what Bella said to me that day," she said, more to herself than for the others.

Her husband stared at her as though confused.

Laurel closed her eyes and recalled the second-grader seeking her out at the end of the school program. Zach knew the story, but she now shared it with Mary.

"Bella approached me after the school's holiday program. She looked up at me, and, with a big smile, declared that I would be a good mother."

A loving smile formed on Zach's face. "She's

right, you know. You're going to be a wonderful mother."

The tears that had been so close to the surface flooded Laurel's eyes, and her throat closed so all that she could manage was a watery smile.

Their caseworker cleared her throat. "Lizzy's parents, John and Abbie, are here. They would like to see you. I wanted to meet with you first to explain a few things before I introduced you."

"I'd like that," Zach said.

Still unable to speak, Laurel nodded.

"Lizzy is with her mother in the labor room, but her father is nearby."

Zach's hand tightened around Laurel's.

Mary took the next several minutes explaining the back story. Lizzy had made the difficult decision that she wasn't emotionally or mentally prepared to raise a child. The baby's father, also a teenager, had signed over his parental rights. As soon as he'd learned Lizzy was pregnant, he'd broken off the relationship and was no longer in the picture. Mary then detailed the terms of the adoption, explaining that Lizzy and her family would prefer an open adoption, which would help Lizzy deal with the grief she'd feel afterward.

The details flew over Laurel's head. She heard everything, but none of it felt real. She felt like she was living in a dream.

When Zach and Mary stood, Laurel did, too. She blindly followed behind them, ready at any minute to pinch herself back into reality. Only after she met Lizzy's father, John Bancroft, did any of it feel real.

"We're sorry to hit you with this news at the last minute," John Bancroft said after exchanging handshakes with Zach and Laurel. "As you can imagine, Lizzy, her mother, and I have struggled with this decision. Once it was made, we needed time to prayerfully consider which family would be best for this baby."

"You chose us?" Laurel whispered.

"Lizzy was the one who chose you to raise her baby. Her youngest sister, Bella, was in your class last year when your first adoption fell through at the last minute."

That seemed like far longer ago than a year. It was another lifetime.

"My wife was a classroom volunteer and she saw how wonderful you were with the children. When you were forced to give up the baby boy, she and Bella witnessed your grief. When Lizzy recently made the decision to put her baby up for adoption, Bella and my wife thought of you, and suggested it to Lizzy."

A nurse appeared and looked over to the caseworker and John Bancroft. "It's getting close."

John focused his attention on Zach and Laurel.

"Lizzy and my wife wanted to know if you'd like to be in the room for the birth."

"Very much," Laurel answered, tears now running down her cheeks.

"Yes," Zach replied with enthusiasm.

The delivery room nurse indicated otherwise.

"Only one of you will be allowed. There's room for two in the delivery room, and Lizzy wants her mother by her side."

Laurel and Zach exchanged glances.

"You go," he said.

Laurel was about to follow the nurse when Zach held her back. Taking hold of her by the shoulders, he touched his forehead against hers and smiled, tears glistening in his eyes. "Welcome our daughter into the world for me," he whispered, his voice breaking.

Laurel nodded, then followed the nurse behind the secure doors.

CHAPTER EIGHTEEN

Mrs. Miracle stayed with Helen for a short time after Laurel and Zach headed off to the hospital. Helen's head was spinning with what had happened. She'd grown impatient with Zach, afraid he was going to ignore the phone call.

"This is it," she said, giving her home companion a high-five, the sound of their hand-slapping echoing through the silent house. "My great-granddaughter is about to be born."

"Are you surprised?"

"Why should I be?" Helen replied with confidence. From what Mrs. Miracle had told her, it would be any day now. She hadn't expected it would be this day, though.

"Shall I make us a cup of tea before you head up to bed?"

"That would be lovely."

Helen made her way to her chair. Once seated,

she closed her eyes and whispered a heartfelt prayer, beginning with a request for the safety of baby and mother during delivery, and that the birth mom and her family would feel comfort in knowing that they'd made the right decision. She then thanked God for sending this special angel to her as a comforter and an encourager. Mrs. Miracle had arrived at the perfect time. She ended by asking God to allow her to live long enough to enjoy her great-granddaughter for a little while.

A few minutes later Mrs. Miracle returned, carrying two delicate cups of tea. "Careful, it's hot," she warned.

Helen held the cup with both hands. She closed her eyes for a moment, reliving the look on her granddaughter's face when Laurel got the news about the baby. She held on to the surprise and joy in her granddaughter's eyes for several moments.

"You knew all along the baby would be born this night, didn't you?" she asked, opening her eyes toward her friend.

"Not exactly," Mrs. Miracle clarified, as she took her normal seat next to Helen. "I knew it would be sooner rather than later, though."

Helen marveled at the timing. "How absolutely perfect that this babe would arrive on Christmas Eve."

Her companion held the cup in front of her and relaxed, lifting her feet onto the ottoman and crossing her ankles. "I couldn't have planned it better myself," she said with a self-satisfied smile.

Helen relaxed against the back of the chair, mull-ing over Pastor Warren's message about the angels visiting the shepherds. "The Christmas Eve service was heavenly," she said to her friend, with a twinkle in her eye.

"Did you enjoy the choir?"

"Oh yes! And no doubt the entire church will be talking about the performance for weeks to come."

"Didn't I tell you it would be angelic?"

Indeed, she had. Helen had one question, though. "I heard Zach mention that one of the choir members was the woman who sold him all those baby clothes that were supposedly on sale. That must have been Mercy. And the bells I heard? Was that when Shirley and Goodness got involved? They added to the voices of the choir?"

"Yes, well . . . my three friends are known to twist the rules. Gabriel attributes every gray hair on his head to them."

"Angels can get gray hairs?"

"Gabriel can," she said with a smile. "Thanks to Shirley, Goodness, and Mercy."

Helen sat and mulled over all that had happened since Mrs. Miracle's arrival. She marveled at all the small hints of a miracle about to happen, and how they had all led to this moment.

"It's a wonder Laurel has yet to believe that God sent you, especially with how clear it all seems to be now."

"I'm not surprised," Mrs. Miracle said, looking thoughtful. "Sometimes humans need a spectacular eye-opener."

"What do you mean by that?"

"One time," Mrs. Miracle shared, "Mercy was working with a pastor whose wife had died. With her death, he'd lost his faith. He was angry with God and unwilling to reconcile his feelings. Mercy desperately wanted to reach him, and so she had to bend the rules."

"How so?"

"He was in church, getting ready for the Sunday service and going about his normal routine, when, against all the rules, Mercy appeared to him in her full glory. Dressed in her shimmering gold gown, she spread her feathery wings and stretched out her arms over him in a total representation of God's love and protective cover provided for the pastor."

"What happened then?"

"He didn't notice her."

"What?" Nana couldn't believe it.

"He walked straight past her without a single acknowledgment of what was right before his eyes."

Helen was amazed at how anyone could be so blind.

Reading her shock, her friend continued. "Actually, it isn't all that unusual. Just look at your granddaughter and her husband. Unfortunately, humans do it all the time, just as this pastor did when Mercy went on full display. He was so caught up in his grief that he was unwilling and unable to see God's love for him."

"Did he ever regain his faith?"

A slow smile emerged. "Oh yes, and once he did, his faith was stronger than ever. In fact, he eventually wrote a book about how Christians deal with grief that became a national bestseller."

This encouraged Helen. "That's wonderful."

"I believe his book is on your bookcase in your room," Mrs. Miracle said. "You read it after Robert's passing."

Helen remembered it now, and the comfort it had given her. How small the world could be, and yet how large heaven must be.

Sipping their tea, they grew silent. Helen had been tired after the service but felt exhilarated and excited after the phone call. Normally, she would be in bed by now, but sleeping was next to impossible.

"Tell me about the baby's birth mother."

"Lizzy Bancroft. She's a lovely teenager, and this decision has been painful, but she's also learned a precious lesson about the incredible gift of motherhood. She'll recover with the help of her parents and move forward in her life. After graduation, she'll stay close to home over the summer and then go to a college nearby so she can watch the baby grow."

"She'll have other children, right?"

"Oh yes. She wants to be a nurse, and after she graduates, she'll meet and marry a nurse anesthetist. Ten years from now she'll give birth again and become a mother of twins, a boy and a girl."

"I'm glad."

Finishing her tea, Mrs. Miracle set the cup aside. "She'll stay in touch with Laurel, Zach, and the baby. Her parents will be a wonderful support to them, also—an extra set of grandparents to the little girl."

Learning these small details delighted Helen, as she most likely wouldn't live long enough to witness all this. At this stage of her life, she marveled at how the days were slow, yet how fast the years seemed to go by.

Mrs. Miracle carried her empty cup into the kitchen. When she returned, she collected Helen's.

"It's time for me to go," she said. "As much as I'd like to stay, Gabriel is waiting to give me another assignment."

Helen wanted to object. She'd miss her home companion, who had now become more like a dear friend. She had no words to adequately thank her. No words to express how much these last few weeks had meant to her. She'd been blessed. God had given her a special gift in this woman.

In this *angel*.

Mrs. Miracle stayed long enough to see Helen to bed. Before she left, the two hugged. *Imagine that,* Helen mused to herself as she settled her head into the pillow. *How many people can claim they've been hugged by an angel?*

In the wee hours of Christmas morning, Helen heard Laurel and Zach arrive back home. Although they'd tried to be quiet, she'd only been half-asleep, longing to hear the details of the birth of her great-granddaughter.

"Laurel?" she called out, anxious for news.

"Nana." Laurel came to the doorway to Helen's

bedroom, framed in the hallway light. "Did we wake you?"

"No, no. I was waiting for you." She sat up in bed and Laurel propped her up with pillows. "Tell me everything."

Laurel sat on the edge of the bed and took hold of her grandmother's hand as she went through all the events of the night.

". . . and I was there in the delivery room when the baby was born. They gave her to Lizzy to hold first," she said, her voice cracking before she could continue. "Then Lizzy kissed her baby girl on the forehead and handed her to me."

"Oh, Laurel." Tears of joy gathered in Helen's eyes.

"Nana, I swear that baby opened her eyes and looked straight into my heart. It was as if she knew I was going to be her mama."

Helen didn't doubt that for a moment. "Of course she did."

"The nurse took her away to measure and weigh. I prayed with Lizzy and her mom, and then Zach and I went to see the baby in the nursery. Lizzy's mom and dad stayed with their daughter."

"Tell me everything," Helen urged.

Laurel straightened, pride glowing from her eyes. "She weighs six pounds, five ounces. She's nineteen inches long. I know some newborns can look terrible following birth, but Nana, I'm telling you—she's beautiful, simply beautiful. Zach and I loved her immediately."

This was exactly how Helen knew it would be. "Have you chosen a name?"

"We had a baby girl's name picked out long ago. Helena Joy."

"Helena Joy," Helen whispered as tears continued to flow down her weathered cheeks. "You named her after *me?*"

"Yes, Nana. After you, and because of all the joy she's given us. I couldn't think of a better name for our daughter. I pray she'll grow into a woman worthy of the heritage of her great-grandmother."

"Oh, Laurel, I hardly know what to say." Helen wrapped her arms around her granddaughter.

They held on to each other for several moments.

"How long did Mrs. Miracle stay?" Laurel asked after they broke apart.

"Only for a short while. You do believe she's an angel now, don't you?"

"I'll believe it, Nana, because you do." The two ladies laughed.

"Hey, you two," Zach said, coming into the bedroom, hearing the giggles. "What's so funny?"

"I've told her all about our new baby girl, and now we're talking about Mrs. Miracle," Laurel said. "Nana continues to believe she's an angel sent by God for us."

Zach grinned. "And your point is?"

"Zach?" Laurel questioned. "Do you really believe she's an angel?"

He looked to Helen and grinned. "How could I not?"

"But . . ."

"There was something I learned in Sunday school many years ago," Zach began to share. "The Holy Book says that we need to keep our eyes open. We can happen upon heavenly beings without ever recognizing who or what they are."

"And you honestly believe this?"

"I do."

"Then if you both believe Mrs. Miracle was God's ambassador to all of us, I'll accept it, too."

"When you bring Helena Joy home, you will," Helen said, taking hold of her granddaughter's hand. "God planned this baby just for you, and Mrs. Miracle was here to prepare you to welcome her into your home and into your hearts."

Her grandmother was right about that. Tiny Helena Joy had already set up camp in her heart.

The next morning, on Christmas Day, Helen's prayer was fulfilled. Laurel and Zach brought her to the hospital to meet her namesake, Helena Joy. The great-grandma wrapped the precious little girl in the soft blanket she had so lovingly knitted in anticipation of the baby's birth. As she kissed the little one's head, Helen could hear the soft sounds of harmonious bells somewhere off in the distance.

EPILOGUE

Five years later

"Helena Joy, smile for your mama," Laurel urged.

"A *big* smile," Zach added from where he stood behind Laurel.

Their daughter stood tall and straight in her pretty red dress in front of the Christmas tree, staring with a hard look at Laurel's camera. Bobby, their year-old son, waddled toward the tree to grab hold of the silvery garland. Zach intercepted the toddler and swept him up in his arms.

"Come on, sweetie," Zach begged his daughter, making a funny face while bouncing Bobby on his hip.

Helena Joy burst into giggles. "Daddy, stop."

"You know how your mama wants a picture of you in front of the tree each Christmas. Cooperate."

Helena Joy covered her mouth and giggled. "I don't want to smile without front teeth."

"Is that what you want for Christmas, Helena Joy?" Zach said teasingly. "There's a song about that, you know."

"Yes, Mama played it for me. I want to go to Disneyland more than I want my teeth."

Laurel lowered the camera. "We'll have to wait and see what Santa brings. Who knows, you might just get your wish."

Their daughter's eyes rounded. "Really?"

Zach chuckled. "You'll just have to wait and see. Now smile!" Helena Joy announced that she hated waiting, and afterward provided a big grin for her mama.

Laurel snapped the photo and then reached for Bobby, taking him away from Zach, distracting the baby with a fluffy stuffed reindeer.

"Come on, little one, it's time for your nap," she said, kissing his pudgy face as he squirmed in her arms.

"I'm too old for naps," Helena Joy stated proudly. "I go to school now."

"Can you help your mama and lie down with your brother? He likes it when you're in the room with him."

"Mama." She groaned.

"Just today," Laurel pleaded. With all the excitement of the holidays, Helena Joy was extra-tired and had fallen asleep at dinnertime two nights in a row. Yes, she was getting too old for naps, but there were days when she still needed one. If she lay down and was quiet for a few minutes, Laurel knew her daughter would soon be fast asleep right along with her little brother.

"Okay."

"Thank you, sweetheart. You're a good helper to your mama." Helena was on her best behavior right before Christmas, wanting to make sure she was in Santa's good graces.

"Before we know it, Bobby will be too old for naps, too." Laurel kissed the top of their adopted son's head as she carried him into the bedroom. He'd been placed in the local foster-care system as a newborn, and they'd taken another emotional risk to foster him in their home. Laurel and Zach loved this little boy from the start, fully aware of the potential consequences—either one of the parents could've claimed the child at any time, if they could prove they were drug- and alcohol-free. It took courage to take in this infant, knowing full well it might result in another loss. Within ten months' time, the parents made the decision to fully surrender their rights to the boy.

After Laurel got the two children settled down, Zach went in to read a book to Helena Joy, although she could have read it on her own.

When the little ones had fallen asleep, as Laurel predicted, Zach returned. She was in the kitchen stirring ingredients for a batch of gingerbread cookies. She baked them every year, just as her grandmother Helen had done.

"You won't believe what just happened," he said, joining her.

"What won't I believe?"

He shook his head and she could read the reluctance in him. He wasn't sure how to explain it himself.

"Just now, while I was reading to the children . . ."

"Yes?"

"You're going to think I'm imagining things."

"You're not the kind of man who is delusional." She set aside her spoon and focused her attention on him.

"I felt the oddest sensation that someone was standing at my side. I looked but there was no one there. All at once, I knew who it was. Laurel, I'm convinced your grandmother stood next to me, watching over our little ones."

"Nana?" Tears instantly filled Laurel's eyes. From the moment Laurel and Zach had brought the baby home from the hospital, Nana had liked nothing better than to rock the sleeping baby in her arms. Nana's health had steadily declined after her great-granddaughter was born, and she had slipped peacefully from her life on earth and into heaven three years after Helena Joy's birth. It was her heart. She'd never complained, never uttered a negative word. She'd accepted that her time was limited. She'd been given all that she had asked of God—to let her live long enough to hold Helena Joy.

"I know it sounds crazy," Zach said.

Tears clogged Laurel's eyes. "No, it doesn't. You know how much she loved little Helena Joy."

"I do."

"I never told you . . ." Laurel said, struggling to hold back the flow of emotion. She sniffled before she continued. "The day we brought Bobby home, I had the same experience. It was like she was there in his room. I wanted to tell you, but I didn't know how to explain it, how to put it into words. I guess I was afraid you'd think I was being overly sentimental or that I was just plain losing it."

"If you're losing it, then I guess we both are." Zach gave Laurel a tight squeeze, then returned to the other room to watch college football.

"I miss you, Nana, more than words can say," Laurel whispered, closing her eyes. "And Mrs. Miracle, if you're listening, I hope you're enjoying a cup of tea with my nana."

Laurel returned to the bowl of cookie dough, and for just an instant she was convinced she heard soft yet distinctive giggles in the distance—the laughter of her nana and Mrs. Miracle.

Love can transform even the best-laid plans
in this heartfelt Christmas novel from
#1 *New York Times* bestselling author
Debbie Macomber.

Jingle All the Way

Continue reading for a preview
Available now from Ballantine Books

CHAPTER ONE

Everly Lancaster was ready to explode. Her assistant, Annette, the very one Jack Campbell, her business partner and CEO, had highly recommended she hire, who also happened to be his niece, had made yet another crucial mistake. One in a long list of costly errors. This time, however, this Gen Z, spoiled, irresponsible, entitled young woman had gone too far.

Annette Howington had mortified Everly in front of five hundred real estate brokers.

"It's really not that big a deal," Annette insisted, smiling as if to suggest this had all been a small misunderstanding. "You did fine without your speech."

The award banquet held in the posh Ritz-Carlton Hotel, a half a block off Chicago's Magnificent Mile, honored the top brokers for the online real estate company Easy Home. As Everly stepped onto the podium to deliver her carefully crafted speech, she discovered that her empty-headed assistant had downloaded the wrong talk and graphics. As a result, Everly had been forced to stumble through what she remembered of it. To her acute embarrassment, she'd sounded ill prepared, fumbling over words and names.

Everly was always at the top of her game. She did not stand up before a crowded banquet room and make a fool of herself.

"Not that big a deal?" Everly repeated, after the banquet. Annette had tried to escape without Everly noticing. No such luck. Everly had the assistant in her sights, and no way was she letting Annette sneak out.

"This is the last straw," Everly said, managing to keep her anger under control. "I've given you every opportunity. I'm afraid I'm going to have to let you go."

"You're firing me?" Annette asked in utter disbelief. "But I'm doing the best I can." For emphasis, she added a loud sniffle. "You've never liked me. From the day I started you've been demanding and critical." Her eyes filled with tears as if that would be enough to convince Everly to change her mind. She sniffled again for extra measure, her shoulders shuddering dramatically.

No way was Everly going to allow Annette to turn this on her. "Your best isn't good enough. You don't possess the skills I need in an assistant. The first thing Monday morning I'll explain to your uncle that you will no longer be working with me or Easy Home." Everly couldn't think of a single position this dittzy girl could manage in the entire company. She'd even managed to mess up answering the phone on more than one occasion.

Annette's tears evaporated and a cocky expression came over her. "Uncle Jack won't let you fire me. I'm his favorite niece."

Everly gritted her teeth. "We'll see about that."

With a confident flounce, Annette whirled around and stormed straight to her mother, who stood in the rear of the ballroom, waiting for her daughter. Everly watched as Annette burst into tears and pointed at Everly. A horrified look came over Louise Campbell as she started to weave her way around the tables toward Everly.

Bring it on, sister, Everly thought, more than prepared to face this tiger mom. Before that happened, however, Everly was waylaid by one of the brokers with a question. When they finished speaking, both Annette and her mother were nowhere to be seen.

Everly had a reputation to protect. She'd worked hard to make Easy Home the success that it was. What Annette said about Jack defending her was a worry, but nothing she couldn't handle.

The problem was Jack and his easygoing, everything-will-take-care-of-itself attitude. They'd met in college while getting their business degrees. Jack was the creative mastermind. Everly possessed the business savvy and drive to take his idea of an online real estate company for Chicago and put it in motion. Six years ago they'd formed a partnership, and, working side by side, the company had grown at a furious rate. With Everly at the helm, overseeing the everyday operations, Jack was content to rest on his laurels after handling the media-facing and investors. Basically, he left the running of the company to Everly. And she'd let him.

First thing Monday morning, Everly approached Jack in his office. "We need to talk about Annette."

Jack barely glanced up from his in-office putting green, where he stood, gauging the distance between the golf ball and the hole.

When he didn't respond, Everly said, "I've given her every opportunity, Jack. I'm letting her go."

Jack, ever willing to overlook his niece's complete lack of professionalism, sighed loudly. "I know. I know. And I appreciate the way you've taken her under your wing. This is my sister's girl and it means the world to Annette to have the chance to learn from you. You realize she idolizes you."

Then God help her if the young woman intentionally had it out for her, Everly mused. "Jack, take your eye off that golf ball and look at me. Favorite niece or not, I'm done."

Jack looked up and his eyes widened. "Annette was named after my mother."

"I don't care if she was named after the Statue of Liberty, I refuse to work with her a minute longer. The girl is incompetent."

His shoulders sagged. "Please reconsider."

That he would ask infuriated Everly. "No."

"No?" Jack looked both crestfallen and shocked. After mentally reciting the alphabet, she tried again. "I know you love Annette and want to please your sister, but I'm the one left to deal with this pampered, entitled, inept girl."

Jack pretended not to hear and did a couple of practice golf swings. "I'll think on it," he said, as if this was his decision.

Which was so Jack. He had tunnel vision and refused to deal with unpleasantness, especially anything having to do with his family.

"Great. You want to keep Annette working here, then I have an idea," Everly said with an exaggeratedly cheerful note. "Make Annette your assistant."

"I can't do that," Jack insisted, leaning against his putter. "Maryann has worked with me from the beginning. Besides, Annette is family." To his credit, Jack looked uncomfortable. When he glanced up, a pleading expression came over his face. Everly knew that look. He was trying to figure out a way to change Everly's mind. That wouldn't work. Not this time.

Jack smiled. "I know you're upset, and you have a right to be. It was a silly mistake, but Annette apologized . . ."

"Silly mistake? She apologized?" If he defended this nitwit one more time, Everly was going to walk out the door and leave the running of the company to him and see what he had to say then.

"You're not listening to me, Jack. I. Have. Reached. My. Limit."

Jack stared at her for a long moment. "I'm pleading with you, Everly. Give her one more chance, that's all I'm asking. With a fresh start I believe Annette will prove her worth. Don't make a hasty decision."

Hasty decision? Had Jack lost his ever-loving mind?

He must have noticed the stubborn expression she wore, because he added, "Remember, this is her first job out of college. We all make mistakes. You did. I did. We were fortunate that people believed in us. Is it so much to ask that we give my sister's daughter the same opportunity?"

"Admit it, Jack, anyone else would have been out the door weeks ago."

"Come on, Everly," Jack pleaded again.

Everly shook her head. "What you fail to realize is that Annette not only let me down, but she's failed you, and this entire organization. You aren't going to be able to turn this around. I'm not changing my mind."

Having had her say, Everly left his office.

Annette sat at her desk, wearing the same cocky look she had at the banquet. The twerp knew her uncle would never fire her, and she thought this made Everly powerless. Everly hadn't built this company and earned the respect of this industry to let some kid win this war.

Jack followed Everly into her office. He paused long enough to close the door before facing her. After a moment, he leaned forward and braced both hands on the edge of her desk. "When was the last time you had a vacation?"

Of all the responses she'd expected from him, this one was a surprise. "A vacation?" she repeated. "What does that have to do with anything?"

"You're stressed out, and it's showing."

"Ya think?" she said with a huff. "I can't and won't tolerate incompetence. If anything, Annette is responsible for upping my stress level." She already had her hand on the phone to connect with HR. Whether Jack liked it or not, Annette was getting fired.

"Letting go of Annette will devastate my sister."

"Your sister?" she repeated, shaking her head. Jack's sister was the least of her worries.

"And Annette, too, of course."

"Apparently you didn't hear me. I gave Annette every opportunity. She doesn't have the skills or the maturity for this position."

"Give her one more chance," he urged, placing his hands in praying position.

Everly adamantly shook her head. "I already have. I've said all I will on the subject."

"It's nearly December."

What did that have to do with any of this? "It doesn't matter, Jack. My mind is made up."

Jack straightened and pointed a finger at her. "I want you to take the entire month of December off."

"What? I can't . . ." It sounded like Jack had lost his mind. No way could he deal with everything if she wasn't around. The entire staff knew she was the problem-solver, not Jack. Then again, maybe this was exactly the lesson he needed.

The idea of sending her away for a month seemed to be growing in his mind as he started to smile, looking pleased with himself. "You need a break and I'm going to see that you get one and that's final."

Everly frowned, wondering what had come over him.

"No buts, Everly. You're too valuable to me and this company, but your drive is smothering your compassion. We'll somehow muddle through without you. Now book a vacation."

Her mouth opened and closed several times before she swallowed. *The entire month of December?* It was November 30; she had no idea where she'd go or what she'd do. Within a matter of days, she'd be bored out of her mind. This position consumed her every waking minute. Then again, there was always email. The team could reach her if necessary. Maybe it wasn't such a bad idea after all to let Jack take over the helm while she silently kept watch in the background.

Before she could stop him, although she wasn't sure she wanted to, he stepped out of the office and went directly over to Annette's desk. "I want you to book a vacation for Everly," he instructed. "Get her a cruise, somewhere tropical, with warm beaches where she can unwind."

Annette snapped to attention. "Right away," she said, eager to please her uncle. She immediately turned to her computer, and her fingers started typing away.

Everly put in a full day at the office. She rarely

left before seven, long after everyone else had headed home. By the time she reached her Chicago condo, it was close to eight. For dinner, she generally picked up take-out on her way home. Her condo had an amazing view of Lake Michigan, although she seldom took time to gaze out the floor-to-ceiling windows. Seeing how little time she spent in her condo, it was more utilitarian than a real home. She had a few framed photos of her family here and there, but other than those, the space could have been a rental. And in fact, at one time it had been, until she was able to pick it up at a bargain price, thanks to Easy Home.

Once she ate her sushi with a glass of white wine, she settled on her white leather sectional and rested her bare feet on the matching ottoman, crossing her ankles. It'd been one hell of a day. She wasn't entirely sure she should take Jack up on his offer. He seemed to feel she needed time away and he wasn't far from wrong. She'd gone six years without a vacation worth mentioning. Oh, there'd been the occasional weekend here and there with her college roommate Lizzy, but those were rare now that Lizzy was married and had a toddler.

Her phone rang and caller ID told her it was her mother. For an instant, Everly was tempted to let it go to voicemail. Then she decided if she didn't answer now, her mother would simply try again later until Everly was forced to answer or be destined to listen to a litany of voicemail messages.

"Hey, Mom," she said.

"Daisy." Just the way her mother said her given

name, which Everly hated, told her her mother wasn't pleased.

"Everything okay?" she asked, ignoring her mother's tone.

"You were missed at Thanksgiving."

Her mother tossed guilt with the expertise of a no-hit pitcher. "I'm sorry, I really am. I thought I could get away, and then at the last minute something came up. I was forced to stay in Chicago and deal with it." She crossed her fingers, hoping her mother wouldn't inquire about that vague *something*. "I did let you know I couldn't make it." Coward that she was, she'd sent a text message.

"Was it the same *something* that prevented you from coming home for Christmas last year?" her mother asked pointedly.

This was the problem. Everly was the middle child in a family of five siblings. Two older sisters named Rose and Lily and two younger brothers, identical twins named Jeff and John. Everly had felt squished in between her sisters and brothers. Rose had Lily and Jeff had John and she was trapped in the middle. Everly needed elbow room, a way to prove she was her own person. She'd set out to do exactly that from the time she was two years old and learned to say the word *no*.

Lily used to tease her and claim Everly had been adopted. She might have believed it except the family resemblance was too strong. She had the same dark brown hair and brown eyes as the rest of her siblings. The same small curve in both her little fingers as all four of her siblings.

Her father blew it off by saying Everly was a typical middle child. Perhaps she was. From her earliest memories she'd been driven to be the best. If her job was to weed a garden row, she did it faster and better than any of her siblings did. She got top grades, was voted the most likely to succeed in her high school class, and was granted a full-ride scholarship to the University of Indiana, graduating magna cum laude. Following graduation, she threw the entire force of her will and determination into getting Easy Home off the ground with Jack Campbell.

In contrast, her two sisters had both married young and started their families, and her brothers had joined their father in the farming enterprise. They had little in common with their up-and-coming-business-executive sister. When she was home it was as if they didn't have anything to talk about. Rose wasn't interested in how exciting the low home mortgage rates were and Everly had a hard time being excited little Rosie was cutting her first tooth.

"Are you going to answer the question?" her mother asked.

"Sorry, Mom, my mind was elsewhere."

"Will you or will you not be home for Christmas?" her mother asked, getting right to the point.

"Ah . . . home." If her family learned that she had the entire month of December off and she skipped the holidays for a second year running, there would be consequences. "I'll be home for sure."

"You promise?"

"Cross my heart. As it is, I'm taking a few days off."

Her words seemed to shock her mother. "You're taking a vacation?"

"That's what I just said."

"You don't sound happy about it."

That much was true. "Jack insisted I needed time away because I'm stressed out and he isn't far from wrong."

"Where do you plan to go?"

"Somewhere tropical, I guess . . . perhaps a cruise." She had never been one to idle away on a beach. The thought of all that wasted time depressed her. She didn't suntan easily and she detested the idea of sweating in a swimsuit.

"You make it sound like you're heading off to Guantánamo."

Everly smiled. "I'm not showing the proper amount of enthusiasm, am I?"

"You're not."

"The thing is, I'm not convinced I should go. Jack isn't as good at the business end of things as I am. I'm worried he'll mess up one or several of the major deals we have in the works."

"Then let him. You've carried your load and his for far too long."

The truth shouldn't feel this sharp. Her mother was right and Everly knew it. She'd gone back and forth on this vacation idea ever since Jack first mentioned it.

"It's up to you to make the most of this opportunity, Daisy," her mother continued. "You can make yourself miserable worrying about Jack and the business, or you can have the time of your life. It's up to you."

They ended the conversation with Everly promising to spend Christmas on the farm and a determination to take her mother's words to heart.

As soon as Everly made an appearance Tuesday morning, Annette hurried to greet her, smiling as if she held a winning lottery ticket in her hand.

"I'm so grateful you've given me this chance to prove myself," Annette said. "Uncle Jack said it was more than I deserve, and I want to thank you." Her eyes sparkled with delight and were as round as the moon.

Everly eyed her warily.

"I found the perfect cruise for you." Annette clapped her hands so excitedly, it surprised Everly she didn't hop up and down. "There was a cancellation at the last minute and I grabbed it. You're going to have such a great time."

"And where is this cruise?"

"Brazil," Annette shouted and thrust her arms in the air as if she were a referee declaring a touchdown.

"Brazil," Everly repeated. *Not bad*.

Her smile deflated a little. "There's only one small problem. It leaves on Saturday."

Everly automatically shook her head. "That's impossible. I'd need shots and to get everything organized here at the office, plus pack." Her head was spinning like a bowling ball heading toward the gutter. No way could she make all that happen.

"That's just it!" Annette declared excitedly. "I've taken care of everything. I've got you an appointment this afternoon for your shots and had the prescription for the malaria pills filled, and"— she stopped to take in a deep breath—"I contacted the Brazilian consulate and they have agreed to expedite your visa application."

Annette clasped her hands and waited as if she expected Everly to applaud.

"Isn't she wonderful," Jack said, coming out of his office. He showed far more enthusiasm than Everly felt was necessary. "This is exactly what the doctor ordered." He smiled at Annette. "Good job."

"Thank you, Uncle Jack. It's refreshing to have someone believe in me." She stared pointedly at Everly.

It demanded effort for Everly not to roll her eyes.

"I'll go first thing on Friday morning to collect the travel documents," Annette said, "so you won't have a single thing to worry about."

The necessary shots were only part of what was needed. "What about my flight?"

"Booked," Annette announced, and shared a high-five with her uncle. "I have you in business class, leaving O'Hare early Friday evening. Timing, unfortunately, is a tiny bit tight, but you should be able to make the ship when it sails Saturday afternoon."

Everly felt like everything was moving far too fast for her to keep up. "This is very last-minute . . .

I'm not sure I can get everything together in such a short amount of time." She needed to get to her desk and handle the most pressing issues herself and delegate the rest. Jack might be her partner, but she didn't trust him to deal with the more stressing aspects of the business. She'd have to monitor him through emails to the members of her staff.

"One last thing," Annette said. "I've got all the paperwork filled out. All I need now is your passport."

"Excellent," Jack said with a wide grin.

For the next three days Everly nearly camped out at her office. She left several of the less delicate matters for Jack to manage. Easygoing Jack had shown far more interest in his golf game than in what was happening with the business. She handled nearly every aspect of the online business, although they were supposed to be partners. The rest of what was on her desk she delegated to her most trusted associates, spending hours explaining what needed to be done and what to expect.

On Friday morning, she woke to a snowstorm. The newscaster predicted ten inches before noon. If her flight was held up because of weather conditions, she would miss the cruise ship.

"What happens if my flight is delayed?" she asked Annette, once she got to the office. "Are there any other options?"

"No," Annette said, as if that had never entered her mind. "I was online searching for quite a while before I was able to find a flight that would get you to the dock on time."

"You did a fine, fine job," Jack complimented his niece, hugging her as if she'd scored an Olympic gold medal in gymnastics rather than managing to book Everly's travel arrangements.

"But the weather," Everly pointed out.

"No worries," Annette said, and handed Everly her travel documents. "I've been assured that the cruise will postpone the embarkation up to three hours if by some chance your flight is delayed. There shouldn't be a problem."

Three hours. She had a three-hour window to make the ship before it set sail.

"Excellent, Annette. You've thought of everything," Jack said, praising his niece yet again. "Brazil is perfect for Everly. Time to laze on a beach, bask in the sun, and let all the stress and worries of the job roll off her shoulders."

Like that was going to happen.

"What are you doing standing here?" Jack asked. "It seems to me you need to get packing. Be sure to stop off at the pharmacy and get sunscreen." He patted Everly on the back and escorted her to the elevator.

With more to do than her mind could comprehend, Everly headed home to pack. Two weeks on a cruise. Her flight was scheduled to fly out at five that afternoon, heading to Manaus, Brazil. According to the documentation, she had two stops and was scheduled to land at noon the following day. The cruise ship was scheduled to depart at three, plus she had that three-hour window if anything went awry.

Back at her condo, Everly pulled out her suitcase and tore through her closet. She needed summer clothes. The problem was her closet was full of business attire. She didn't own a single pair of shorts.

Everly detested all this rushing, afraid she would miss packing something vital. This wasn't the way she operated. She liked to plan everything out well in advance so she could be in control, but that option had been taken away from her. With only a few hours left to get ready, she packed what she thought would suffice, determined that she would shop for anything she needed once she arrived in Brazil.

By the time she left her condo the gently falling snow had turned into blizzard conditions. When she arrived at O'Hare, she discovered her flight had been delayed an hour. Fine, if the flight was canceled, then she had the perfect excuse to remain in town. Jack couldn't fault her for the weather. Already she was having second thoughts about leaving him in charge.

With nothing to do while she waited for her flight, she sat at the bar sipping wine, waiting for the latest update from the airlines. Two and a half hours after her scheduled departure time, her flight was called.

CHAPTER TWO

After two glasses of wine on an empty stomach, Everly was eager to close her eyes and do her best to relax. As much as possible she put the tight schedule out of her mind. If she missed the cruise, she missed the cruise.

At check-in she got the information for the two plane changes. One in Atlanta and another in São Paulo. She'd been assured by the airlines that there wouldn't be a problem with her connections, as she had a three-hour layover in Atlanta. Everly didn't want to dwell on how close she was cutting it to reach the ship on time. Already her mind was coming up with a contingency plan. If she missed the cruise, she would simply rent a hotel room and spend the next two weeks shopping, keeping in touch with everyone via email. She'd downloaded three business-type books she intended to read, so there would be plenty to occupy her mind. And for a guilty pleasure, she downloaded several romances as well.

As it turned out, she missed the connecting flight in Atlanta, but there was another flight leaving in two hours. That had an effect on the flight out of São Paulo as well. Thankfully, the airlines were able to find her a connection with a different airline that had her landing two hours into her three-hour window. The possibility of her missing this cruise was beginning to seem real. It would be tight, which would make the long overnight flight to Brazil too stressful to sleep.

Once she was on the plane in Atlanta, the woman sitting next to her in business class glanced over and smiled. The two struck up a conversation and Everly enjoyed chatting with another business executive. They had a lot in common. The flight attendant delivered them each a glass of champagne and a dinner menu before the flight's departure. Ah, the luxury of it. At least Annette had gotten this part right.

"To a safe flight," Heidi Johnson, her seatmate, said, and they clicked glasses.

Everly sipped the bubbly and sighed. "Are you able to sleep on these long flights?" she asked her companion.

"Not a problem."

This was encouraging news. "I'm stressed about making this cruise." Everly hated the thought of arriving in Brazil half brain dead from fatigue.

Heidi leaned her head close to Everly. "I have a little helper that puts me right to sleep."

Everly was interested. "What is it?" she asked.

Digging inside her purse, Heidi held up a small bottle of sleep aids, saying, "I take one of these little jewels. They work every time."

"I've never taken a sleeping pill." It was a rare night that Everly couldn't sleep.

"These knock me out in nothing flat and I sleep like a baby. By the time we land, I'm as fresh as a daisy."

Everly wished she'd thought ahead enough to have considered a sleeping pill. With so little time to get ready, she'd scrambled to pack, buy what she needed as best she could, and get to the airport in time for her flight. She felt breathless remembering rushing around her condo, grabbing clothes and stuffing everything in a lone suitcase. She did manage to pick up sunscreen and a few other necessities, but that was it. Never had she felt more ill prepared. Heaving a sigh, she told herself it would all work out in the end.

"The seats make up into a reasonably comfortable bed," Heidi told her. "Would you like one of my pills?"

"I would. Thanks." If Everly was going to arrive in Manaus with a functioning brain, sleep would certainly be helpful. Besides, what was she going to do with herself for the next ten hours if she couldn't sleep?

Her newfound friend handed over the small pill, which Everly downed with the remainder of her champagne. When the attendant came to collect her dinner order, she ordered the pasta, which was surprisingly tasty, along with another glass of wine. By the time her dinner tray was removed, she was yawning. The sleeping aid had done its job in quick order, and Everly was grateful. She thanked Heidi again.

With the help of the flight attendant, Everly lowered her seat to the reclining position, laid her head down on the soft pillow, and closed her eyes. The lights in the cabin dimmed. Almost immediately she could feel herself drift off into the wonderful land of dreams.

Soon her head was whirling with the most fanciful visions, to the point that she was unsure if she was asleep or awake. She sighed as she saw herself walking along a sandy beach in her bikini with a full-length sheer coverup blowing behind her in the wind. The warm, gentle waves of the Brazilian waters rippled against her bare feet as her footsteps left indentations in the wet sand. Admiring looks from other sun worshipers came her way as the wind tossed her soft brown hair about her face. With her head tilted toward the sun, she basked in the approving glow of admiration.

At five-ten, she was the tallest of the three Lancaster girls. As a kid she was all legs. Her height had helped her in the business world, she felt, and she used it to her advantage, often wearing three- and four-inch heels. No man was going to intimidate her. She wore her thick shoulder-length hair straight, often securing it at her nape.

She wasn't looking for a relationship for the simple reason she didn't have time for one. Driven as she was to make Easy Home a success, she found her work week often included twelve-hour days and often exceeded sixty hours a week. She was the first to arrive in the mornings and the last to leave. Her role in the company had taken over her life. Jack was right: She was stressed. What Everly needed was a life, a real life that involved relationships, laughter, and social events. All of which were sadly lacking. She couldn't even remember the last time she'd been on a date. Well, actually, she could. It was the night Dave broke up with her, claiming she was married to her job.

A vacation, she reasoned, in her half-dreamlike state, would be the perfect time for a romantic fling. A smile curved the edges of her mouth as she contemplated meeting the man of her dreams.

A fiery Latin lover. Ooh la la.

The cruise should give her ample opportunity to meet men. It was sure to be a romantically rich environment. Everly's dream was getting better by the minute. She pictured herself in the arms of a dashing man worthy of being a cover model. His muscles bulged as he bent her backward for a toe-curling kiss, sweeping her off her feet.

And then the lights came on.

Everly blinked against the brightness and pushed the button that would raise her bed into a sitting position. Rubbing her eyes, she heard the pilot announce that the plane would be landing in São Paulo within the next hour.

No sooner had she finished speaking then the flight attendant came down the aisle with a cart, offering coffee.

Everly continued to blink. It felt as if she was

caught in a thick fog and was drifting outside her body.

Placing her hands over her face, she shook her head to clear her vision and wake up. It astonished her to learn she'd been asleep for nearly eight hours. It hadn't felt as if any time had passed at all. The last thing she remembered was her romantic fling with a Latin lover.

The flight attendant handed her a hot cup of coffee, which she eagerly downed, hoping that would help clear her head. She stared into the brew after each sip, as if the cup contained the answers to the universe and the solar system.

Her seatmate must have noticed her difficulty. "Are you having trouble waking up?"

"I . . . I don't know. I have the funniest feeling . . . like I'm in the middle . . . of a sandstorm." It sounded as if someone else was speaking. Everly hoped she wasn't slurring her words and feared she had.

The woman laughed lightly, as if she found the situation humorous.

Everly looked at Heidi, but it wasn't the same Heidi she'd spent the first part of the flight with. This woman resembled a demonic creature who was laughing maniacally, as if Everly had sold her soul by swallowing that pill. She blinked and shook her head again and the original Heidi reappeared. Sighing with relief, she sagged against the back of the seat.

"Didn't I tell you these pills work every time?"

"You did." Everly kept her gaze straight forward,

for fear Heidi would return to the unearthly creature from earlier.

"You've got to love drugs," Heidi said.

Horrified at what she might have digested, Everly swiveled her head to look at the other woman and asked in a slurred voice, "What . . . did you . . . give me?"

"Nothing illegal, just a normal sleeping pill. It hits people funny sometimes. No worries, it will all wear off in a few hours."

The flight attendant came by and collected the coffee mug and the plane was readied for landing. The Boeing 767 took a hard bounce against the tarmac and eventually coasted to the jetway.

Although she continued to feel like she was having an out-of-body experience, Everly exited the plane. She staggered a few steps, as if she'd been on a drinking binge, and nearly lost her balance. Perhaps it was mixing the sleeping pill with the alcohol that was responsible for this side effect.

Once in the airport, she needed to get through customs and find the gate to her connecting flight that would take her to Manaus. She'd never heard of the city, which was clearly somewhere on the coast. People were talking around her and it was the oddest thing. Their words made no sense. It was as if the letters had stacked themselves on top of one another like building blocks. Even though she strained to make sense of what was being said, she couldn't understand a word, until she realized no one was speaking English.

She was punch-drunk, hardly able to remain upright and unable to understand a word anyone said to her. Fumbling in her purse, she reached for her boarding pass and realized that because of her missed flights, not only was she changing planes, she was changing airlines as well. Stymied, she froze, completely overwhelmed, unsure what to do.

As if in answer to a prayer, a man pushing an empty wheelchair rolled past her. Frantically she waved her arm until she got his attention. Without help she didn't have a snowball's chance of making this flight, let alone the cruise.

Before he could object, she awkwardly fell into the chair and handed him her boarding pass. Once he had it, she thrust her arm straight out and shouted, "Forward."

Good thing she did, because the gate was a good half-mile from where she'd cleared customs. Her head continued to whirl around as if she were caught up in a tornado, and she clenched her purse like it was Toto. Only she wasn't in Kansas, although it felt like she'd landed somewhere over the rainbow.

Wheeling past one gate after another, Everly continued to blink, hoping that would help to clear her vision. The connection was tight, and if not for the ride, it was unlikely she would have made the flight on time.

It helped that she was in business class. She was even more grateful when the flight attendant greeted her in English. "Is there anything I can get you?" he asked.

"Coffee, please."

Within a few minutes he returned with a fresh cup of coffee.

Grateful, Everly drank it with the hope it would help clear her head. "We're going to Manaus, correct?" The last thing she needed was to board the wrong flight.

"That's right."

"I've never heard of this city." World geography wasn't her strong suit.

"Really? It's famous."

"It's fairly large, then."

"Oh yes, I think the population is well over two million."

"Really?" That was a surprise. For the last six years, her focus was on real estate in the States. She could name nearly every county of more than ten states. But ask her to point out Liechtenstein on a map and she was clueless.

The attendant had to move on to ready the plane for departure, cutting off their brief conversation.

Just when everything seemed to be coming together there was a problem with the airplane, and they were delayed thirty minutes, which cut the time to make the cruise even tighter. Everly couldn't think about it. If she missed the cruise, then so be it. Even though she was nervous, she quickly fell asleep and woke as it was announced that they were about to depart on the four-hour flight to Manaus. She could fret or she could sleep. Sleep chose her. Leaning her head back, Everly slipped into dreamland as if she hadn't a care in the world. This must be the way

Jack felt all the time, carefree. Lighthearted, with a devil-may-care attitude.

By the time the plane landed she was almost back to normal. Checking the time, she saw that she had twenty minutes left of her three-hour leeway. Rushing to baggage claim, she got her suitcase and shot out of the terminal to catch a cab.

It took her five tries before she found a driver who was relatively fluent in English. "I need to get to the cruise dock, pronto." She read off the name of the pier from her travel document. "The ship is waiting for me . . . at least I hope it is. I'll give you double your normal fare if you get me there quickly." She swatted at the mosquito buzzing around in the cab's interior.

The words hadn't left her lips when the driver pulled away from the curb, wheels screeching, leaving rubber behind. Everly tumbled across the seat when he made a wild turn. Once she righted herself, she grabbed hold of the seatbelt and tried unsuccessfully to lock it into place. The mosquito wasn't helping matters any. The pesky fellow wouldn't leave her alone.

"Your first time Manaus?" he asked as he sped through a red light.

Hanging on to the seat in front of her with both hands, Everly nodded. "First time."

"You not see Opera House?"

"You have an opera house?"

"Very famous."

"Perhaps another time," she said, as she slid all

the way across the backseat as he took another crazy turn. It felt as if the vehicle had gone up on two wheels. Everly let out a cry of alarm, which didn't seem to concern the driver.

"Come see fish market, too."

"Okay. Sure." Not in this lifetime. Everly intensely disliked the smell of dead fish.

"Where you from in America?" he asked.

"Chicago."

How he was able to drive like he was Vin Diesel in *The Fast and the Furious* and carry on a conversation baffled Everly.

"I've got cousins in Chicago."

"Have you been there?"

"No, only California in Cabo San Lucas."

"That's Mexico."

Taking his eyes off the road, he swiveled his head around to look at her. "You sure?"

"Yes, quite sure."

"Funny, my cousin doesn't think so."

"Is this the same cousin in Chicago?"

"No different cousin."

Everly noticed they were in an industrial area of the city. Soon afterward, the cabbie slammed on his brakes so hard, she was nearly catapulted over the seat next to the driver. Breathing as hard as if she'd completed a marathon, she reached inside her purse and handed her driver a fistful of money. He beamed her a smile and helped her out of the car. Grabbing her suitcase, he held on to her elbow as they speed-walked to the gangway.

A man was standing just inside the ship. "Are you Daisy Lancaster?" he shouted.

Hearing her given name gave her pause. Naturally the ship would have the same name that was on her passport. "Yes," she shouted back.

"Good." He held out his arm and helped her up the last few steps. "Welcome aboard," he said. "Glad you made it."

The cabbie handed off her suitcase to the ship's steward. He took it and smiled approvingly at Everly. "I have always appreciated a woman who could pack light."

She smiled dryly. "Am I the last one to board?"

"You are." He reached for a phone and issued instructions to the crew before he said, "I'll escort you to your stateroom."

"Thank you." That was kind of him, and she dutifully followed him to the elevator. As they exited, she heard the ship's horn as the vessel prepared to leave the dock. Because of the rush, she hadn't paid much notice to the ship itself. Now that she was aboard, it was much smaller than what she'd anticipated.

Her stateroom wasn't anything to brag about, either. She stood in the doorway, shocked at how utilitarian it was. A bed and a nightstand and a door that led to the bathroom. There was a small desk with a chair, too. "This is my room?" she asked, doing her best to hide her dismay.

"Yes, top deck. You were lucky to get it, as we had a last-minute cancellation."

Everly remembered Annette excitedly explaining

that she was fortunate to have found a ship with space at this late date.

"Do you have my room key?" she asked.

The steward met her gaze. "There are no locks on the stateroom doors."

"No locks?" she repeated, certain she hadn't heard him correctly.

"That's correct. None of the staterooms have locks."

Looking around, she noticed several other standard items one would expect were missing as well. "No phones?"

"No."

"Television?"

"None of those, either."

"In any of the staterooms?"

"That's correct."

A cold feeling settled over her, chilling her to the bone. She held her breath and then asked the one question that was a matter of life or death. "What about Internet access?"

"Afraid not."

Horrified, Everly sank onto the bed. "I need the Internet."

"I'm sorry, Miss, the answers to all your questions are in the brochure, including the fact there's no Internet while on board."

What brochure? Annette seemed to have conveniently forgotten to include that. "You don't understand. I can't function without the Internet." She would need to speak to the captain immediately. "What kind of luxury cruise is this?"

"Luxury cruise?" he repeated, shaking his head. "Lady, this is the *Amazon Explorer*."

Everly blinked, certain she hadn't heard him correctly. "Are you telling me I'm on a cruise going down the Amazon River?"

"That's exactly what I'm telling you."

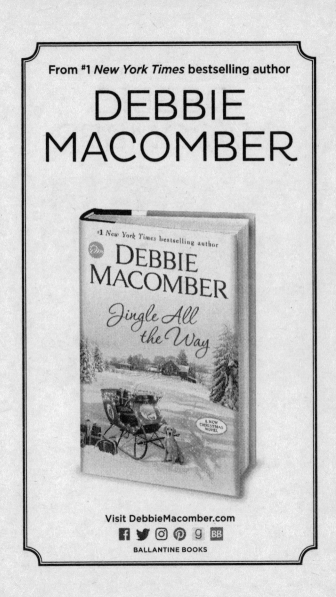